One Hundred and Sixty-four Buttons

By Gregory John Ferris

TRUDY	Matriarch of the Button family
JILL	Middle-aged daughter of Trudy
DANIELLE	Great niece of Trudy, 20-30 years of age
BRENT	20ish boyfriend of Danielle
TRACIE	Female cousin, 30ish
GEORGE	Middle-aged nephew of Trudy
TUCKER	12 year old boy cousin, George's grandson
MORGAN	12 year old girl cousin

SETTING

A family reunion on a large farm in central Pennsylvania
Summer 2017

Act I scene 1 mid-morning farmhouse parlor
Act I scene 2 mid-morning farmhouse porch
Act I scene 3 30 minutes later porch
Act I scene 4   20 minutes later, porch
Act I scene 5   a few hours later, porch

Act II scene 1 immediately after, porch
Act II scene 2 front yard, later the same afternoon
Act II scene 3 immediately after, porch
Act II scene 4 front yard, a little later the same day
Act II scene 5 porch, late afternoon

SCENE 1

(Farm house parlor, old furniture, piano, various end tables, monochrome photos of ancestors on the wall, along with a color portrait, much more recent, of an ill, emaciated woman, and a topographic map pinned to another wall).

BRENT

And what about this one, Mrs. Button, the one with a label?

JILL

I won't tell you again, Brent, my name is Jill, not Mrs. Button. This is a reunion, not a corporate business meeting. My married name is Portier, anyway, we women give up so much to marry. Danielle, you need to teach your boyfriend to follow instructions better. Otherwise, he won't last very long.

DANIELLE

Oh, the whole family is very familiar with that button, Brent. Anyone could recount its history.

BRENT

I couldn't honey. This is such a beautiful parlor Jill, it must be the heart of the Button family.

DANIELLE

Thank you. Yes it is the heart. They say that walls has ears, but these have eyes as well. The parlor may be the heart but the stomach will be arriving here soon here en masse. We should have over 150 attendees this year. I never know until they either show or don't show. You'd think that a French family would understand RSVP, but after centuries in America, I guess that is too much to expect. As far as this button with a label, it belonged to Nips.

BRENT

The Nips? As in the Japanese?

DANIELLE

No, it's a nickname for my Uncle Cornelius. That was quite a mouthful of a name, so he went by Nips. And this is a button from his WW2 uniform.

BRENT

So he fought against the Japanese? Nips was an insult for them, wasn't it?

JILL

Maybe, I don't know. So many wars, they seem to do nothing but disrupt family lives. But Cornelius' nickname came from a childhood candy or cookie. It had nothing to do with the war or the Japanese. Brent, in our family, we don't disparage strangers or foreigners; we prefer to mock other members of the clan. No, not that clan, Brent. Clan as in family. Jeez, one has to be so sensitive when you meet someone these days. People are just precious little newborn chicks.

BRENT

Don't worry Jill, I'm not made of porcelain.

JILL

Great. As I was saying, insults too valuable to waste on people who don't appreciate them.

DANIELLE

It would be like serving good wine to strangers. Although today we won't be serving good wine to anyone, I suppose, if Uncle Bert brings his home brew. Is he?

JILL

Yes, I'm afraid so. He called to let me know that he'd be bringing plenty of filled jugs, so that I wouldn't have to worry about buying any foreign wine.

BRENT

No foreign wine? You mean that there won't be any French wine at a French reunion?

DANIELLE

By foreign, Bert means outside of the county. He's proven the world wrong in being able to grow grapes and produce wine in the hills of Pennsylvania, but so far his efforts haven't got him his photograph on Wine magazine.

BRENT

Your other uncle, Nips, did he die in the war? I see that the label has the address of the White House written on it, and what is this, one of those forever stamps stapled to it. There has to be a story with this button.

JILL

Well, everyone, everyone except you, knows the story of this military button, probably because of the label. Uncle Nips went to war, in Europe, but before leaving he left a button from his uniform for the family. He promised that he would post it to the government upon his return, I guess he considered that leaving something undone was a good luck charm. And, if by chance, or lack of it, he didn't return, a family member could drop it in the mail for him.

His mother, my grandmother, believed that it gave him an obligation to fulfill, a reason to survive the war.

BRENT

I see.

JILL

It sounds stupid doesn't it? Superstitious.

BRENT

(*Pause*) Nips' button is still here. So he never posted it.

JILL

No, he never posted it.

BRENT

So, he did not return? Alive, that is?

DANIELLE

No, he returned, safe and sound. He lived a good life and passed away 40 years later. That is over 30 years ago now; it's fading into ancient history. But we still have his button. You could say that it served its purpose.

It's funny, he was always a stickler for the rules; he was a part of that generation. Each year, around Memorial Day, he would verify that the postage on the label was sufficient to return the button to who he claimed was still its rightful owner.

All of the lost and destroyed equipment in that war, not to speak of the dead and maimed, and Nips wanted to assure that his button was only considered burrowed, not stolen. As if a misplaced button was at the top of US government priorities.

BRENT

That sounds like someone very devoted. You mentioned that he passed over 30 years. What will become of the button, now that he isn't here to return it?

JILL

Well, as you can see, we attached a forever stamp to the label and so the onus is now on the federal government. They've promised to honor the forever stamp, well, forever, and our family has promised to return it before forever happens. The FBI haven't been around making inquiries, and so, for now, Nips' button remains in the box. (*Horn honks*)

DANIELLE

Well, more guests are beginning to arrive. And it has to be cousin Joyce Bouton, you remember that she went back to using the French version of button. I swear, she honks only to announce her arrival like some sort of medieval herald.

JILL

They're not guests Danielle, they are family, even Joyce. Stay here with Brent, and enjoy a few minutes of peace before the storm. (*Jill exits*)

DANIELLE

These buttons represent us and tell a story of each of us. They come from uniforms, wedding dresses, anything in fact. We share and reuse them, they can be like books in a library. They have stories added to them, it seem a bit Halloweenish at first.

BRENT

An entire family preserved in a cigar box

DANIELLE

They can be carried as good luck charms, even as a necklace. You could call them fetishes, I suppose, but it's more than that.

BRENT

They are all different, you couldn't make any one piece of clothing from these.

DANIELLE

No, only a family.

Buttons used to be handmade, each was almost unique. They are constructed from bone, wood, ivory, I guess ivory is no longer employed, but really anything could serve as material.

Oh, I really like this one (*retrieving a small silver broach in the shape and design of a feather from the box*)

BRENT

Why, is that one yours?

DANIELLE

No, you found my button months ago; don't you remember? I do.

BRENT

Oh, aren't you the witty one? (*kiss*).   I meant a button among these ones.

DANIELLE

I'll let you guess later which one is mine. But I'll only give you three chances. This one, does it look familiar, Brent?   Look around carefully.

BRENT

Hmmm, no, it's not really a button, it's more like jewelry, something that would be worn…

DANIELLE

Yes, worn. As Aunt Lydia is doing in her portrait, see? With Aunt Lydia, life was art. She lived her life as if she had written each scene only moments before, with no time for rehearsals.   She would have been a huge success on Broadway, but she never gave it a glance. Real stages weren't real to her, Broadway would have been too small and confining for her.

BRENT

Her portrait is quite powerful.

DANIELLE

Haunting?

BRENT

No, I wouldn't term it haunting, although others might find it disturbing, even unworldly. No, I'd describe it as honest. Who painted it?

DANIELLE

Her son, Doug. I really hope that he shows up today, he always comes to these reunions, even if I don't attend. He is so much fun. I hope too, that you like him.

BRENT

Doug is a painter? And one of your cousins is a playwright?

DANIELLE

Yes, that would be George, that's a good name for a writer, I think. But so is Doug, a playwright I mean. He has one about Santa getting into an accident with a texting driver, it's hilarious. But painting and sketching are his true gifts.

BRENT

Your family is full of artists.   But why this portrait of his mother? It's…uh.. a bit somber, maybe even…

DANIELLE

When Lydia was very sick, terminal to be blunt, Doug stayed with his mother in Paris. He made portraits of the dying; his mother and other patients in a hospital in Paris. It may have just started as sketches, something to do with his hands and eyes when there was nothing left for him to say with his lips. The patients were mostly women. Men don't seem to linger. Or it may be that men have no vanity.

BRENT

Obviously, you don't know men as well as you let on.

DANIELLE

Do you think that men are more likely to accept it when a doctor, usually a man, passes a death sentence on them? They hear the doctor's word and take it as a personal command, and poof, a few weeks later, the male patient is gone.

BRENT

I don't know, I don't dwell on death, dead, dying, or demise. Really, very few of the the D words are in my vocabulary. I prefer life, living, lust, and

. DANIELLE

Love?

BRENT

Lunch.

DANIELLE

I think that women would ignore their male doctors in a similar case. They are used to men lying to them, or if not lying to them, are used to men being wrong. Don't you agree?

BRENT

You've posed a question that is impossible for any man to answer correctly. Bravo.

DANIELLE

All of the portraits and sketches, this one included, were done quickly.

BRENT

I'd expect so.

DANIELLE

That is not what I meant. Not everything uttered requires a clever response. (*pause*) Sorry, it's just that Lydia was so full of life and laughter, she was too open to be clever, too kind to appreciate barbed repartee.

BRENT

I'm the one who is sorry, Danielle. I meant..

DANIELLE

They were done, as, oh, what is the word? I have no artistic ability, so I don't know the jargon. They were color sketches that captured the moment, but they'd be perfected later in oil or acrylic.

BRENT

I still don't understand. Why would someone sit for such an unflattering image? Were they blind, were your aunt and these other women lying to themselves, devoid of all emotion except vanity? What is your conclusion? You knew her, I didn't.

DANIELLE

In my opinion, it was for love.

BRENT

Love?

DANIELLE

Yes, love of life, of being able to still participate. And gratitude. Gratitude to the one person, even a stranger, who still wanted to spend time with them, someone who accepted them as they were. Someone who found them interesting, and who, in capturing their final days, assured them that they were still alive.

(*Morgan and Tucker rush in, murmur hellos, and then spot and move towards map on the wall*)

Anyway, that is her story, and this is her button. Pretty isn't it? Her remains were cremated in Paris but here in this room, holding this, I have no doubt that a part of her hovers around us today in the air.

(*George enters, hugs Danielle, and is introduced to Brent*)

GEORGE

I heard you talking about Lydia. It's a shame that her son Doug won't be here today.

DANIELLE

Oh, don't tell me that. What happened? This is so disappointing

GEORGE

He decided to stay in Paris a little longer. If I were in his position, I'd have chosen Paris over Punxatawney as well. I'm disappointed as well, Danielle. It's a shame that we only see each other every few years. Doug is so funny. He brings as much life to these reunions as his mother.

DANIELLE

See Brent, I told you that Doug is funny. George, have you come to visit your button?

GEORGE

Guilty as charged. Brent, many of us come to check on them every reunion. It's not my button, but Charlie's.   Let me tell you about him.

Hey kid, are you my grandchild? Kids all look alike don't they (*one is clearly a girl, the other is clearly a boy*), just like the young say that all old people resemble each other.

DANIELLE

Your grandfather is going to tell us about Charlie. I love this story.

GEORGE

Charlie's is the smallest button in our family box. Being so small he is usually found underneath the others, and ignored by most of those searching for their own memories.   In particular, the children pay him little attention. Would you have noticed him?

MORGAN and TUCKER

No, it's tiny, and so plain. I like that one better.

GEORGE

 You are like a crow Tucker, attracted to big, bright things. Charlie is the runt, the ugly duckling. He isn't ugly of course, but he is small, yes, plain, and overlooked.

BRENT

It looks modern, is it from a child?

GEORGE

Hmmm, let's see. Is it the fastener from the clothing of a child, or from a woman's lamb skin glove, or from the sleeve of an ornate shirt handmade for a gentleman? It could be any of these, or none of them.

This button belonged to Charlie even though he never wore it.   He was just a cat. For 17 of his 19 years he lived with us, with me. Being constantly in the house, he was the closest thing to a full time friend and companion that I had, especially after the death of my wife.

My wife's death was sudden and unexpected, while Charlie's was slow and expected. He was a friend, an adopted member of my small immediate family.   The button box is supposed to immortalize family members and what is, or was, important to them. Charlie was important to me, Brent. Telling this button's story opens me to either your praise or ridicule, for you are an unbiased judge, while Charlie, well, he was just a cat.

What you hold in your hand is from one of my dress shirts. They say to render garments in such circumstances. That means to tear your clothes, Tucker. I buried him in that shirt, keeping only this one small, white relic, which I hoped everyone would overlook when I placed it in this box, because he was just a cat.

To be honest, I was afraid that some members of the family would object, pointing out correctly that Charlie was not really a blood relation.   He was just a cat.

I underestimated my family. When the cat button, as some called it, became known, no one objected, they even suggested that we replace it with a larger, more normal size button, but that wouldn't be right, would it?

So, now Charlie is in the box with the others, but he doesn't hide any longer. And with my story told, I hope you rule your honor, that Charlie is no longer, just a cat. (*Morgan leaves, followed by Tucker*)

BRENT

That is a sad story, George.

GEORGE

It would be even sadder if it were true.

BRENT

It's not true?   But you told it so convincingly.

DANIELLE

George is a writer. Each of the buttons here has a story, so are true and some are false.
Some are both.   Charlie's button is true.

BRENT

How can anything, let alone a family story, be both true and false?

DANIELLE

We like the truth but we like stories better. Good stories are always true.

GEORGE

I remember vividly how Charlie would watch out the window overlooking the driveway to the garage, waiting patiently my return. After his death, I noticed that a spider had spun a web on the outside, no longer deterred from doing so by a large vigilant guard. I left the web undisturbed. Its presence reminded me of his absence. I missed him more than her.

BRENT

Her, the spider?

DANIELLE

You could say that and not be wrong.

GEORGE

I wasn't Charlie's first owner.

BRENT

It said that cats don't have owners. (*pause*)   Is this part two of Charlie's true story? (*pause*) Yours was not his first home, then?

GEORGE

No. I've come to realize that I do better in second hand relationships. It must be the result of being the youngest child, hand me downs become the norm.

DANIELLE

I thought as much, I've heard tales about your late wife from some of the family. Wasn't she a hand me down also? (*pause*) Did I just say that out loud? It's like I can't not speak aloud when I'm with these mute buttons.

BRENT

Does your late wife have a button as well, George   (*George and Danielle regard each other and burst into laughter*). What did I say? This is going to be a long day for me, I can see that now. You two, and all the others that I'm going to meet, have the home field advantage.

DANIELLE

His late wife.

BRENT

Yes, that is what I said.

DANIELLE

His late wife turned out to be too early.

GEORGE

I didn't want to say this front of the kid, Tucker can be the sensitive sort, he's only, well I'm not sure exactly how old he is, around twelve or so, but when I put my cat Charlie down it was the most unpleasant thing I ever had to do. And believe me, I'd had my share of unpleasantness. But murdering my wife was among the most pleasant.

BRENT

What? You murdered your wife?

DANIELLE

Her name was Sophie.

GEORGE

Her name was Shannon.

DANIELLE

I only knew her as Sophie.   He had her killed.

BRENT

This is another family joke, isn't it?

DANIELLE

Yes, and no. This all happened before I was born, or maybe when I was still a child. Do you want to tell it, George?

GEORGE

No, not at all. Please, continue.

DANIELLE

It all began at one of these family gatherings, a reunions, or was it a wedding? Yes, one of the family reunions, thanks. Anyway, George was already here at the farm, and Shannon..

BRENT

Shannon, not Sophie? This is already confusing. This is going to be a very long day.

DANIELLE

You'll understand in a minute, Brent. I promise.   So, Shannon shows up with another man, who she introduces as a friend, but it's clear that he is much more than a friend.   It must have been awkward beyond belief. I'm surprised that the boyfriend had the courage to attend, but apparently he'd been told that it was just a party, not a family reunion, where his girlfriend's husband, let alone his whole family, would be present.   What she did was an in your face insult to the entire family.

BRENT

Jill told me that your « clan » enjoyed insults. (*Danielle frowns*)

GEORGE

Shannon always did enjoy drama.   Her actions were quite theatrical, better than any breakup scene that I've written, I'll give her that.

BRENT

What happened next?

DANIELLE

What you might expect.   Shannon and the boyfriend, no one seemed to remember his name in the excitement, left soon after arriving.   She had brought him as a prop to announce the upcoming divorce, she could have simply used the US mail as any other normal soon to be ex-wife. It would have been kinder…

GEORGE

Kindness and courtesy were in short supply with her…

DANIELLE

And George left shortly thereafter. To plan either his suicide or her murder were the leading bets; with most of the family coming down on the side of murder. They were already coordinating his alibi. The family was as angry as he was.   And they were right. The divorce came to pass, and a few months later, George's first mystery novel was brought out in print. The book was very successful. Which is why I said his late wife left too early.

BRENT

And the murder of Sophie or Shannon, you got away with it?

GEORGE

Yes. I was actually lauded for killing her. Don't look so concerned, it was only in print, Brent, only in print. Shannon became Sophie in my book, and is of course, murdered. I really enjoyed that.

DANIELLE

The whole family recognized the Sophie character as Shannon of course. It became quite popular to read sections of it, really, just the murder scene, after dusk, at each reunion. I'm sure that you can find a copy in one of the bookcases in the parlor. I remember that we'd have a reading from the bible before the reunion dinner, and a reading from George's « Late to the Reunion » before we roasted marshmallows.

GEORGE

I mentioned my cat, Charlie. With cats, the world is all about them, but they are honest in their narcissism. Shannon or Sophie, sometimes I can't remember which one was the wife and which one was my creature; neither was upfront in dealing with me or anyone else. The profits from the book more than made up for my losses in the divorce.

BRENT

What became of the real wife and the boyfriend?

DANIELLE

She tried to return and restart with you, didn't she, George?   But you told her that you didn't do rewrites in real life, or something equally pithy.   That is what I heard.

GEORGE

Close enough.   But I did bring the murdered wife back in another mystery. I'd had such fun in murdering her once that I did it a second time.   That book sold even better than the first (*laughs*). Women readers really seemed to enjoy it for some reason.

I wonder if my readers would accept me bringing her back for a third time. That might constitute overkill, if you'll pardon the pun.

BRENT

The boy who left a few minutes ago, Tucker, is he actually your grandson?

GEORGE

Yes, but honestly, I'm a poor excuse for a grandfather. I wasn't a very good dad either.   My late wife and I had a daughter together, but I raised her poorly, or perhaps she was too much like her mother.   In either case, it was my responsibility and I failed at it. Mary, that's her name, her mother was adamant about assigning our daughter a simple moniker, I think that was another sign of her ego.   She didn't want her own daughter to pull the spotlight away from herself, and so she strapped Mary with an ordinary name.

Mary is divorced now, that's ordinary enough as well these days. She and her ex-husband Tyler married young but not for long, about the same length as her mother and I were, now that I find myself talking to you about it. After the marriage, she discovered what she called true love, by which she meant sex, and he joined the military, where he found hate in true war. Each is happy now, I think, Tyler is really a great guy, but he's more married to war than he ever was to Mary. So, it's me and..

DANIELLE

Tucker, George. You grandson is named Tucker.

GEORGE

See what a poor parent I am, I sometimes forget that I have a grandson, let alone his name. I can't blame it on Alzheimer's, I've been checked. Funny isn't it, I can remember the name of a long dead stranger's disease that I don't have and that I don't want, but not the name of a grandson that I do have..

DANIELLE

And that you do want? (*George shrugs*)

GEORGE

So, Brent, you'll not find a button for my wife. Excuse me now, I should go see if Jill needs a hand with anything. I'm sure that we'll have a chance to talk more later. I need to hear your stories instead of rehashing mine. (*exits*)

BRENT

Well, that was interesting. Going forward, I'm not sure if I should believe anything that I hear or see here today. Danielle, do you think that your cousin George is bipolar?

DANIELLE

I certainly hope so. If not, he'd just be crazy. (*Brent and Danielle exit*)

Morgan and Tucker enter and go to map on wall, which Tuckers removes, folds and places in pocket during the conversation.

TUCKER

See, I told you. There it is, marked on the map, Morgan's Rock. It must be huge to be on a map.

MORGAN

You're right. It must be named for another Morgan.

TUCKER

It doesn't matter, once we get there, it becomes yours. And with the map it will be easy, I even found a compass in the shop. Maybe I will find a big rock and claim it for myself. These rocks are like boulders or miniature mountains. Tucker's boulder is a great name. We only have to cross this stream.

MORGAN

Is there a bridge?

TUCKER

Sure there is a bridge. Who would build a stream without a bridge? No one, that's who. What good would it be?

MORGAN

The fish in the stream? They don't need a bridge

TUCKER

You don't know fish at all Morgan. They love bridges.

MORGAN

You're wrong Tucker, fish don't cross bridges.

TUCKER

You're the stupid one. They like bridges because of the shade. And they like the bugs that are unlucky or clumsy enough to fall in from the bridge. I hope that you are not clumsy Morgan. And the biggest fish like stupid kids who don't know that fish like bridges, yeah, kids like you who don't know anything about fish or bridges. The fish hide and eat anything that falls in.
 In the winter they kinda hibernate under the ice, so you'd be safe if you fell in during the winter. You'd die from freezing to death, but you wouldn't be eaten by the fish until spring when the fish woke up. The fish like fresh food but they'd eat you anyway once you'd thawed out, they can eat like a bear.
 And if the fish didn't get you, then the real bears would when they woke up from their hibernation

MORGAN

This is July. I should be safe from freezing today. So who built the bridge?
 If you're so smart about them, tell me who built it.

TUCKER

Hunters built it and take care of it. If you were lucky some hunters might find you if you did fall off the bridge in the wintertime. They would have to cut off your leg, maybe even both of them, cause they'd be frostbitten. They would leave them in the water, you wouldn't need them after the hunters just cut them off. And in the spring, they would be there for the fish.

MORGAN

You're just saying all of this to scare me.   And this is still July, Tucker.

TUCKER

Well you can just stay here then, I don't care.   You can stay with the witch's picture (*points at portrait on wall*).   Maybe she will come and get you. (*turns to leave*)

MORGAN

Who is she? She must be a relative.

TUCKER

She might be your real mother. Most kids at these reunions are adopted. I'm one of the few who aren't someone else's kid. I'm a real Button.

MORGAN

She is not,   I know what my real mom looks like, she's outside. I'm a real Button, too.

TUCKER

She looks like she could be your mom   And see looks like you, too.

MORGAN

No, she doesn't. My mom is young, and she's not a witch.

TUCKER

You heard what cousin Danielle said, that they burned this woman and that part of her is floating around here.   They only burn witches, and only witches can fly. They must have burned her for being wicked. Danielle said that they burned her in Paris, they do it all the time over there. The place is just full of witches.

MORGAN

Was she really a witch? You are just making things up. You tell stories that aren't true. They aren't very good either. I thought that you were going to take me to Morgan's rock. But you are just telling foolish stories. (*looks back to portrait*) She just looks sick. But she is pretty too, pretty for being old and sick.

TUCKER

I don't care. I'm leaving soon, and you can come along or not. If the bridge is still there, I'm going to cross it. If it has been washed away in a flood, I can swim. Can you swim? (*Morgan nods*) Good. If not..

MORGAN

I know, the fish would eat my legs. What if it floods when we get to the bridge?

TUCKER

It won't, it's not even cloudy. And after the bridge, we can climb some giant rocks, huge boulders bigger than this house..

MORGAN

I don't know, maybe..

TUCKER

Maybe what? Mom told me that Grandma did this when she was a kid.

MORGAN

She did?

TUCKER

I don't know, I don't think so. But I understand what my mother means; if an adult did something as a kid, that means we can do it too. See, you just have to translate what adults say into what they mean. When they grow up they forget how to say things in our language. So are you coming along with me or not?

(*Both exit*)

SCENE 2

(*Farm house porch, Jill and Danielle listen as cousin Tracie recounts one of her recent stories*)

JILL

Here comes Tracie, you remember her. Her first husband was…

DANIELLE

You're not going to be nasty are you?

JILL

No, of course not.

DANIELLE

Oh, why not? I wish for once that you would be nasty. I'm sure that you'd excel at it. Won't you at least give it a try? For me? If you're not good at nasty, I can give you some tips, remember I was the head of my sorority.

JILL

You, mean? You're as sweet as honey, Danielle. Just for you, I could attempt it just this once.   But if I'm as talented at being cruel as you hope that I will be?

DANIELLE

I said nasty, not cruel. I'll settle for either, though. Tracie's first husband, what was his name? Harold?

JILL

No that doesn't sound correct. He was too young to be a Harold and too stuffy to be a Harry.

DANIELLE

This is not going to progress very far if neither of us can remember anything. Wait, his name was Kenny.

JILL

Yes, it was. I remember now, Kenny. Lenny was the other cousin's loser husband. I always got the two of them mixed up.

Lenny's favorite pastime was watching television. I don't understand how anyone could spend so many hours staring at a screen. For him it was sports, nothing but sports. It drives me crazy, just thinking about that. He didn't or couldn't work. He lived, I use the term loosely, he lived as if he were in solitary confinement for the greater part of his existence.

Now, Tracie's husband Kenny, he was ok, pretty quiet, but goodness was he cheap, really cheap. We used to call him Penny Kenny behind his back. (*Tracie enters stage left*)

TRACIE

Hi, it looks like another great turnout, Jill. Trudy is still looking her wonderful, healthy self. She's always the same.

JILL

She is slowing down, I'm surprised that you haven't noticed. Mom must be putting on a special effort for the reunion. I hope she hasn't doubled up on her medication for this occasion. She quit taking it weeks ago, but may decide to restart it today. If so, she'll sleep all day tomorrow.

DANIELLE

You don't appear to be slowing down either. You haven't brought your latest boyfriend. Or are you in between them?

TRACIE

I've been in between boyfriends several times, Danielle. It can be invigorating. You should try it yourself.

DANIELLE

We were just talking about your first ex, Kenny.

TRACIE

That must have been the shortest and most boring conversation on record. Although I do have my one favorite story about Lloyd. It's not totally family friendly, so to speak. Say, Danielle, where is your boyfriend? I'd like to meet him.

DANIELLE

Oh, Brent is around here somewhere. He's probably playing horseshoes or softball.

TRACIE

So another man who likes sports. We absolutely we need more of those. Softball was never really my sport. But Brent is a great name. Don't you wish that when we married we had a custom of changing the name?

JILL

But we do, Tracie. You changed your name when you married. I was at the wedding. But wait, I thought you married Kenny. Who is Lloyd?

TRACIE

No, changing the husband's name after marriage. That's what I did. Kenny became Lloyd. That was my secret name for him.

DANIELLE

Did he like it?

TRACIE

Not at all, I tried it once or twice and then just kept it to myself. I just don't care for the name Kenny, it reminded me of a good, stable, electrician. A decent provider.

JILL

But he was an electrician. He wasn't that bad, you describe him like an insurance policy.

TRACIE

I don't know, I still prefer Lloyd, it has more zip, more elegance. Or even Brent. I remember one time, we went to Washington, DC. Of course Lloyd had to take all his camera equipment, as if none of the sights had ever been photographed before by anyone.

DANIELLE

I remember now, wasn't Lloyd pursuing art as a second career?

TRACIE

Yes. Unfortunately, he never came close to capturing it. Toward the end, he went abstract. In more ways than one. He should have spent more effort in pursuing me. *(pause)*. So, he took all of these photos. Photos of me in front of some building or other, next to some statue. You know, the sort of thing that everyone does.

DANIELLE

That's what tourists do in the capital.

TRACIE

He considered his photography art. I guess he thought that once he'd married a Button, he would absorb some artistic talent from me somehow. Boy, was he mistaken. *(pause)*. It turned out that I'm only artistic in bed, and Lloyd didn't have much of a brush.

After he was gone, I got rid of most of his photographs.

DANIELLE

Except for those taken in Washington?

TRACIE

No, including those. If I'd thought about it at the time, we could have done a fashion shoot instead of me wearing the same drab outfit in every picture. I could have even included some risqué shots. We could have entitled it Cherry Blossoms in DC.

JILL

That would surely have added some zip to the trip.

TRACIE

Oh well, it's too late now. At the time, Lloyd was so annoyed that the Washington monument was closed indefinitely. Something to do with a broken elevator. My unartistic husband thought there was some nationally important omen in its closure.

JILL

Only a man would see an omen. A woman would see a broken elevator and have it fixed.
Men build these grand monuments to one another, but they never want to vacuum up afterwards. Men do that, they are so impractical. They don't see reality in the same light as women. For men, it's a never ending quest for something.

TRACIE

For me it's the right shade of blue in a size six with a tapered 2 1/2 inch heel.

DANIELLE

Boys don't outgrow their fixation with superheroes, while they don't even maintain their own physiques. Men most want they aren't.

TRACIE

It's lucky for you that you learned that lesson early. What men aren't doesn't matter. What they are lazy pigs with silly visions. Some clean up pretty good though, even for pigs.

JILL

She's right, you know. Only a man could invent such a crazy idea as all these competing, all powerful gods, and then blame women for the subsequent disasters.

DANIELLE

I don't know, maybe that is the way it used to be. Some men have moved on to believing in sports. I see these new faith symbols in the rear windows of cars, 13.1, 26.2.

TRACIE

I thought that those were some bible reference. I don't play religion, myself. I left Purgatory at puberty.

DANIELLE

And went straight to hell, if the stories are true.

JILL

They are references of a new obsession. At least in sports men don't have to wait thousands of years to be disappointed.

DANIELLE

And they can have a beer during the service.

JILL

Sport is just so boring, the same action over and over and over.

TRACIE

That can be relaxing, don't you think?

JILL

In my opinion, sports is too scripted and predictable. They even change the regulations when someone is injured. How manly is that? Really, what adventure can happen on a half-acre manicured lawn, observed by 50,000 drunks, and cameras everywhere? At least my late husband was not a sports fanatic, he played golf once every six or seven years. He was like a cicada in that respect.

TRACIE

He sounds like Lloyd and sex.

DANIELLE

Is this your one good story about Kenny? I mean Lloyd. Let's hear it. There aren't any children around.

TRACIE

Sex and the seven year cycle. Lloyd was such a miser. He rationed everything. Thank goodness that the bus hit him early in his seven year cycle. Hmm, he was smashed just a cicada. I had hoped that it would be another way, but he was too good of an electrician to fry himself. It turns out that it was me who was the live wire.

I would have liked to have had an open casket for him. But the imprint left by the bus's grill made that impossible. He resembled one of those unhappy celebrities forced to sell some unpronounceable medicine on television.

Right before they closed the coffin's lid in the back of the funeral home, I slipped a picture of the tall, erect, Washington monument in the casket with him.   I figured it would give him something to reflect on. To be fair to Lloyd, I did learn one thing from him.

JILL

Men usually have much more than one lesson to teach women. Or so I've been taught.

TRACIE

Lloyd liked to play golf, much more than Paul did.   Lloyd was a very good golfer, he informed me of that often enough. In fact, he always shot par.

DANIELLE

That's impossible. Unless he cheated. Oh, I see. So if he cheated, while he was on the green, you were playing through off the green?

TRACIE

I wouldn't say that. Not then. What I meant is that after each stroke,

DANIELLE

Stop! I need a full glass before you continue. (*pours herself wine or another beverage*).

TRACIE

After each club stroke, each golf club stroke, he would proceed to where he intended the ball to be, not where it actually landed, or in his case, where it watered. He called it a uni-scramble. He said that playing that way took a lot of balls.

JILL

I'm sure it did.

TRACIE

But he was willing to use balls that weren't his. He'd used whichever ones he found here and there. Boy, was he cheap. Just a real miser.

DANIELLE

Oh, really? I never knew that about him (*looks at Jill*) Did you?

TRACIE

That was his defining characteristic. Anyway, I really took that statement to heart. It was his one male lesson that made sense to me. If he as a man was willing to use balls that weren't his, then I, as a mere woman, if I ever wanted to golf, should be willing to use balls that weren't his as well.

JILL

So, Tracie, you mentioned that you're unattached for the moment. What else is new with you? I'm surprised that you're here alone; there aren't many prospects at a family reunion.

TRACIE

No, I'm just a bit exhausted.

DANIELLE

So, you are slowing down.

TRACIE

Maybe, I'll let you two be the judge. I was dating an older man, Bruce. Older men are easier to please, and less clingy. Take my word for it Danielle, not every woman has access to a teenager as you do. What time is his curfew?

DANIELLE

He's 21.

TRACIE

21? I see. He looks very young.

DANIELLE

Brent is 21 years old.

TRACIE

So, older men, they don't want to stay awake all night. I end up in bed but not in bed with my end up.

JILL

Who is this Bruce?

TRACIE

He isn't anyone. He died. It happened at dinner in an expensive French restaurant in Atlanta. They are famous for their incredible chocolate dessert, a pot de crème.

JILL

I always found French cuisine too rich for me.

TRACIE

If the man paying is rich enough, you don't notice the cuisine. And if the woman is beautiful enough, nor does he. Normally, Bruce is, was, a quiet guy. He was one of those men you consider somewhat like a pet. You know, how with a cat that can be quiet and cuddly, and can be trusted to use an indoor bathroom? So, I didn't really notice that sometime during the meal, he'd stopped eating and responding to conversation. I reached across the table and took his hand, that was easy enough to do, and I felt for a pulse. Nothing. He was just sitting there, a bit slumped forward, D E A D, dead.

JILL

What did the waiter say?

TRACIE

Well nothing. It was a waitress, I remember because she was cute. So many thoughts ran through my head. I needed to think, so, first I ordered a cognac, they had a very good selection. It was VSOP, if I'm not mistaken.

DANIELLE

That's usually ordered after dessert, isn't it? I know about dining in public. I didn't waste my college experience after all.

TRACIE

Probably, I guess, but as I said, I needed to think. People don't usually die between courses. I'm not sure which dinner protocol needs to be followed exactly in such circumstances. I was in shock.

DANIELLE

And then, afterwards, did the police arrive?

TRACIE

Danielle, please let me explain events my way. This is my story, not your interrogation.

DANIELLE

Ok, Ok, sorry. I only asked a logical question

JILL

You know better that to attempt logic with Tracie.

TRACIE

I drank the cognac, but I think the waitress had made an error.

JILL

In what way?

TRACIE

I think that she gave me an XO instead of a VSOP. I wasn't quite sure if she'd passed me an XO as some type of code, if you know what i mean, (*Jill shakes head no, Danielle nods yes*) or whether it was just bad service. I really expected better, given the restaurant's prices. It was just so confusing.

DANIELLE

Having a patron die in a restaurant would be confusing.

TRACIE

It wasn't that, the waitress hadn't noticed Bruce's passing. It was just that a party of eight or so nearby was singing happy birthday, in French. I sat there, a bit sad. I felt bad that Bruce wouldn't have another birthday, and I a little mad about the inferior cognac. Then, I remembered that I probably would have another one, have a birthday that is. And then I thought that Bruce had probably expected to have another one too.

DANIELLE

You were doing a lot of thinking for someone in shock. You should try shock more often.

TRACIE

You know, thinking about it now, I'm not in shock today Danielle, I bet that the good cognac went to the birthday table by mistake. It's too late to complain, but I should give them a bad review anyway.

JILL

Sure, why not? That sounds like a reasonable thing to do.

TRACIE

Ok Jill, I hear your sarcasm. I'll skip the review, but I really wanted to try the chocolate pot de crème. I didn't know when or even if I'd ever return to that restaurant. Did I tell you that it was expensive?

JILL

Please don't tell that me that you ordered yourself dessert, instead of informing the manager of Bruce's death?

DANIELLE

Or calling for the paramedics.

TRACIE

No, I would never behave so callously.

JILL

You wouldn't behave callously? Why, was this during Lent? Or you didn't behave callously?

TRACIE

Both. I wouldn't and I didn't. I ordered dessert for the both of us.

DANIELLE

But he was dead. D E A D, dead!

TRACIE

Danielle that was no justification for me to be rude. I couldn't just order one. You just told me that you learned about dining etiquette in college.

DANIELLE

The courses I took didn't cover what to do in the case of dead dinner dates. They were lacking in that regard. It must be my turn to write a bad review.

TRACIE

Of course I had to finish his, with his being dead and,

JILL

And what else?

TRACIE

Well, I guess dead was reason enough. The good news is that the pot de crème was as wonderful as it had been described to me by a girlfriend.

DANIELLE

Maybe I'll try it the first time that I am in Atlanta.

JILL

So finally you let someone know about Bruce?

TRACIE

Indirectly, yes.

JILL

I fear understanding what the word indirectly means in your universe.

TRACIE

I asked the waitress to call the manager, I didn't give a reason, and when she strolled away, I wasn't too in shock to notice that she had a gorgeous, round derriere. The shock was wearing off a bit, I suppose.

JILL

Mine isn't.

TRACIE

I remember thinking at the time, I should have got her phone number. You know waitresses in nice restaurants don't wear name tags. I was going to ask her if she enjoyed lake time, but I couldn't do that in front of Bruce.

JILL

Excuse me, what is lake time? (*Danielle leans over and whispers in Jill's ear. Jill has look of shock*). Oh, I see.

TRACIE

You should try it some time, Jill. Darn, I won't be able to go back to that restaurant again, will I? So, the waitress went to fetch the manager, and I left.

DANIELLE

You left? You just left.

TRACIE

Of course. Otherwise, I'd have been stuck with the bill. Did I tell you that the restaurant was expensive? And Bruce, he'd had nearly half of the meal,

DANIELLE

Including cognac

TRACIE

It was his responsibility. The restaurant was his idea.

JILL

You just said that it was your idea.

TRACIE

I did say that, yes you are correct. But it was Bruce's idea to agree with me. So, he should have paid for it. It was his responsibility.

DANIELLE

Including dessert.

TRACIE

That's right. If he hadn't been there, I wouldn't have ordered one for him. In hindsight, I was wrong, I made a mistake.

JILL

There is hope for you, after all. You went back later to pay the bill?

DANIELLE

Or to ask about lake time?

TRACIE

No, I meant that I had made a mistake about the meal. Bruce had hardly touched his main course.

DANIELLE

Because he was dead.

TRACIE

Well, yes. Still, even so, I should have requested a doggie bag. It's a shame, we had the same taste when it came to food.

JILL

Did you attend his funeral?

TRACIE

In a way. Yes and no.

JILL

This is going to be another convoluted story, cousin.

DANIELLE

You love her stories as much as I do. Admit it.

JILL

You're right. Heaven help me, but I do. Tracie your stories are so believable in their unbelievability.

DANIELLE

They're augmented with alcohol. Providing a nymphomaniac with alcohol always ends with an epic like this. Like the one about with the equipment failure in Geneva..

TRACIE

Alcohol is an adjective to life. Bruce taught me that one. I like it. It's called an axiom.

JILL

A little booze can go a long way. A little more just screws things up.

TRACIE

So I was entering the church...

JILL

Wait, so we are back on track in the original Bruce dies at dinner movie? Good. Ok, so you are at his funeral (*Tracie nods yes*) Which denomination? Or was Bruce Jewish?

TRACIE

How would I know? Those types of buildings are all the same, with some sincerely smug jerk standing in front, wearing a funny costume. I've found that those sorts make the worst lovers. They only understand how to please themselves. They don't get partnerships.

DANIELLE

You certainly...

TRACIE

I'm amazed that they don't say oh me, oh me, when they... I certainly what?

DANIELLE

I don't know. You just derailed my train of thought.

JILL

I agree, she certainly.

TRACIE

So, I met this cute guy walking into the funeral.

JILL

Undoubtedly someone the age of your son, if you had one. About the same age as Brent?

TRACIE

Probably. Young with plenty of stamina. We skipped the service; death begets lust, as the good book says.

DANIELLE

It does?

JILL

We must not have the current edition of that book, dear cousin. If we had internet here, I'd check Amazon this very minute.

TRACIE

I suggested a shower to him, one can never be too clean to be dirty. We did it two or was it three times? That's stamina for you, girls.

JILL

You are so nasty!

DANIELLE

Finally, we get to nasty.

TRACIE

That's what he said. During the interval.

DANIELLE

Interval?

JILL

She must mean intermission.

DANIELLE

Is that what you call it? I've only ever been in one act plays. Often, just one scene, really just a brief monologue. Maybe with Brent I'll have a leading role

JILL

At least you had a role.

TRACIE

You would have been right at home with Bruce. Yes, that's right, intermission. During the intermission, will you be upset if I say during the first intermission, there were several, I asked him how he knew Bruce.

JILL

Does him have a name?

TRACIE

I'm sure he does, it that important?

JILL

Apparently not.

DANIELLE

And how did him know Bruce?

TRACIE

It was strange. We were fated to meet, it seems.

JILL

How so?

TRACIE

Well, he was the first paramedic on the scene at the French restaurant where Bruce had his last foie gras.

JILL

Oh I see that Joyce has dressed for the occasion, but I haven't spotted any entourage. I swear that she is competing with cousin Merl, except that where Merl acquires a new career, Joyce acquires a new husband I asked her once about prudence and tolerance and she replied, "Those sisters died years ago" We talked about remodeling at the last reunion. I said that she had remodeled more times than I can count, I've only done it once.

TRACIE

If you are going to talk about my mother in front of me, you can at least be polite and say things that aren't true. A white lie is always welcome.

DANIELLE

How did Joyce answer you Jill?

JILL

She said that I was mistaken, that I counted wrong, and that when it came to remodeling it was the same for the both of us, it's been once per husband.

DANIELLE

Joyce is so glamorous.

TRACIE

Unlike this one (*indicating Tucker*). Where are you off to, Tucker? You won't need a backpack for the family scavenger hunt, Jack will provide bags for both teams.

TUCKER

I'm not playing that stupid game. We're supposed to search for things that we already have? This is a waste of time. It's no different than an Easter egg hunt. Without candy. How stupid.

JILL

Your father used to really enjoy these games. One of the hidden items might even be his. It will be fun.

TUCKER

I already have enough of his things at home. I miss him.

JILL

So do I. Maybe not as much as you, but a lot.

TUCKER

I wish that he'd never left.

JILL

So do I, Tucker. We all do.

DANIELLE

You father was angry Tucker, but not at you. (*to the women*) They have a curve, like a ball in flight I think.

JILL

The word is trajectory. But I have no idea what you mean.

TRACIE

Curve or trajectory, all I know is that once on the ground men just lay there like slugs. And their so called flight time is usually overrated.

DANIELLE

Their emotions overrule their minds for decades. And then they claim that women are hormonal, too moody. Men are just permanently angry. They remain primed and set like an exploded bomb; ready to destroy the tranquility of an innocent passersby.

TUCKER

I know about bombs, I see videos on YouTube.

JILL

Men outgrow it anger, they mature. Some do.

TRACIE

Mature men, what a joke. They are like drones.

TUCKER

I know about drones too, Tracie. They're good for blowing up terrorists. I saw videos.

JILL

My God, what a world.

TUCKER

And for sports, I like the Tour de France.

JILL

Listen to that; bombs to drones to biking. It's all the same to him, YouTube equalizes everything. Seeing everything is believing everything. Evil is no longer the enemy, it has become just another search category.

DANIELLE

A very popular one, I suspect.

JILL

Turning off the internet is like self-admitting to rehab. The pleasure of unplugging has become a medical necessity.

TRACIE

So what is the bag for then, Tucker, if not for the scavenger hunt?

TUCKER

We're going to hike to Morgan's rock. Like Grandma did.

TRACIE

Hiking in the woods? Like Grandma did. That's crazy.

TUCKER

She's not crazy, she's just not the same as us.

TRACIE

That's for sure. It is dangerous.

TUCKER

Grandma isn't either a kid, or a grownup. She must be what people become at a certain age.

TRACIE

Which is what?

TUCKER

I don't know, but it's what Grandma is. We need to leave now. Bye.

DANIELLE

Take that, Tracie. The king has spoken, "We are going to hike to Morgan's rock". How cute.

TRACIE

And who is we, Tucker?

TUCKER

Morgan and me, duh. Who else would want to go to Morgan's rock?

TRACIE

Indeed, who else?   Well if you'll excuse me, I'm going to see the rock that Joyce is speaking to. He's quite the hunk.

JILL

That's Brent, isn't it, Danielle?

TRACIE

I like that name, it is even more masculine than Lloyd. I'll need to introduce myself. Bye now. (*exits stage left*)

JILL

Well, Tucker, you had better check with your father, I'm sorry, your grandfather, about this hike of yours. He won't like you going off alone.

TUCKER

He'd just say no, so there is no reason to ask him.

DANIELLE

He might say yes. He might even go along with you.

TUCKER

Yeah, right. He won't. He never does. Maybe if I was a book, he'd want to spend time with me. You grownups force me to read books, stories about adventures with boys like me. Why? You just end up telling me no, I can't do anything like those boys. I can't do this at home. I'm old enough to do things by myself now; all the best things happen to us when we are twelve.

DANIELLE

Who told you that?

TUCKER

All the old guys, you can ask them yourselves. Even gramps would tell you. I think that it makes the old men sad, wishing that they could be twelve years old again.

DANIELLE

And how old are you now Tucker? Twelve?

TUCKER

Yep. Me and Morgan are both twelve this year.

DANIELLE

Even twelve year olds need parental control.

TUCKER

Parental controls? Mine can't even control themselves. Do you see either of them here?

JILL

Danielle, you need to pay attention to your own non twelve year old. Tracie and Joyce have your boyfriend surrounded. Joyce may not have an entourage, but Brent sure does.

DANIELLE

I need to speak with Brent anyway, about his upcoming conversation with Grandma. You know what those interviews are like.

JILL

You need to talk with him about several things, Danielle. Your young boyfriend certainly has a wolfish side, but you may need to rescue him from the tigress and the cougar.

Danielle exits stage left, and a moment later, Jill exits stage right.

MORGAN

Tucker, is your mom divorced? Why are you at the reunion? You're not a true Button.

TUCKER

Yeah, she is. And I am as much a Button as you are. Just like everyone here.

MORGAN

Where is your dad? Why isn't he here?

TUCKER

My dad is at the war.

MORGAN

Which one?

TUCKER

I don't know, his war. The one over there.

MORGAN

Where? Over there?

TUCKER

Yes, the war over there. I don't know for sure, but the one the soldiers go to is over there. Is it important to know where?

MORGAN

No, I suppose not. Are we winning?

TUCKER

Sure, we must be winning. Soldiers go there all the time. Adults claim say that children need constant attention and watching so that we don't get hurt. The best advice for kids is to beware of their parents.

MORGAN

I'm ready now to leave now, Tucker. Are you sure this is safe?

TUCKER

Pretty safe, Morgan. And if it isn't safe, I have this. (*opens bag for Morgan to peer inside, and then they exit stage left*).

SCENE 3

BRENT

Your family has quite a place here.

DANIELLE

Everything that you see, as far as you can see, has been in the family for over a century.   100 years is not very long in Europe, but here it is an eternity.

BRENT

Speaking of what a person can see, I was talking to Joyce. She is your...?

DANIELLE

She is everybody's.

BRENT

What?

DANIELLE

Surely you picked up on it?

BRENT

Well...

DANIELLE

You're a young, well youngish man, virile, you have enough miles on you to have surmised that her odometer has been reset more than once.

BRENT

I was going to say..

DANIELLE

That she comes across as a nymphomaniac?

BRENT

Not that necessarily..

DANIELLE

She does because she is. She really can't help it, it's a disease. It's one of the few diseases where the victim is blamed for having it. You should be safe here with me, if its safety that you want. Is it?

BRENT

What does that mean? Your family knows that we're an item. But safety is not the only thing I want in life.

DANIELLE

I want to be more than half an item. Half an item is something found in the bargain basement.

BRENT

We're not married, we are not even engaged yet. You may think that I'm auditioning for your family, but's it mutual. This is more like an in depth, executive job interview. Where else would I meet so many of your family in one place with their guard down? At the reception it would be too late.

DANIELLE

Reception? We are that far down the path?

BRENT

Your family's invitation tells me that we are heading in that direction. I wouldn't say that it's on the horizon, but I've seen the signposts for it. This is another one.

DANIELLE

So on this road trip of ours, are there exits ahead?

BRENT

There are two drivers in this car, so sure. We either arrive there together, or not at all.

DANIELLE

So what are you looking for? Pretend that you aren't madly in love with me and tell me the truth.

BRENT

I'd tell you the truth anyway.

DANIELLE

That isn't a very good answer. Truthfulness is a worthless quality in a man. I'm glad that it isn't your predominant one. Lies can be much better, or at least sweeter, like freshly picked apples. Way over there is the apple orchard that my great something grandmother planted. We still collect apples from it in the fall and store them in the barn. Some of the trees have died of course, and the wooden outbuildings come and go. Wood is only dried flesh, says Trudy. Whatever can't be maintained or preserved can be rebuilt. Me, I like to think that everything, on the farm, trees, buildings, animals, all of this constitutes the real family. I'm rambling, but it's soothing to describe this farm to someone, a stranger, not that you're a stranger of course, but this is all new to you. Describing this to you is like seeing it again for the first time myself. So?

BRENT

So? So, what am I looking for? Insanity, to begin with. (*pause*) Your family's craziness not mine. Families bring their best behaved skeletons to family reunions.

DANIELLE

Ancestry.com is not welcome here.

BRENT

Too many skeletons in the closets?

DANIELLE

No, the house is short on closets, we use a nearby wetland. What is one more strange smell in a swamp?

BRENT

Did anyone die in this house? Which room?

DANIELLE

Maybe, I'm not sure. Not many. They're not still there. That's for the best, it is only a three bedroom

BRENT

Your reunion is my best chance to observe a representative cross section of your tribe.

DANIELLE

You are very scientific about this.

BRENT

I am. I take this very seriously. I could be at a Yankee's game right now.

DANIELLE

The Yankees aren't doing well this year, their bullpen is weak.

BRENT

I didn't know that you followed baseball.

DANIELLE

I don't. But everyone's bullpen is always weak. In and out of baseball. Cousin Joyce will tell you that, and I don't think she's ever struck out.

BRENT

This courtship thing is like ordering an unfamiliar dish in a new restaurant. It is cheaper than engaging, sorry, engaging is a poor word choice, cheaper than hiring either a professional match maker or a private investigator.

DANIELLE

I take it that you've done both. You've hired matchmakers and investigators?

BRENT

Yes, but that can be expensive. But not with you, Danielle. I've also tried social media, which is anything but. It fails without fail. I'm hopeful that this method is more dispassionate.

DANIELLE

I see. Dispassionate. That's not the first word that comes to mind when I think of courtship. Well, now that you've selected your clinical, dispassionate, process, how do you choose your first subject? Do you need my help? Or do you leave it to chance?

BRENT

I'm afraid it is too late for that, I've already met at least four of your relatives, 6 if you count the bipolar ones twice, and my Button virginity is no longer intact.
Your assistance might skew results. Don't worry, I'll blend in. I usually leave my lab coat in the car, it raises suspicions.

DANIELLE

Usually? So you've done this before?

BRENT

Once or twice, even once for a colleague. I had to charge for that, transportation and such. I could have billed him a nonfinders fee; her family should have been placed on the no fly list without exception. They were odd enough to merit their own reality tv program.

DANIELLE

I don't believe this, Brent. You're taking what little fun is here and crushing it in the dirt like a cigarette butt.

BRENT

Don't worry, I'm only kidding. About the money unusual. You haven't tried this yourself?

DANIELLE

No, but you've given me a wonderful idea. If my family passes your personal investigation then, no, better yet, even if we fail spectacularly, you must promise to take me to meet yours, skeletons and freaks included. Fair is fair.

BRENT

Good. I promise. You're catching on. I like that.... a lot.

DANIELLE

I'm a quick study. Did you meet my cousin who dresses very bizarrely? (*pointing*)

BRENT

Yes, I did. It's refreshing to know exactly who you meant when you described her. She is the only one in leopard skin. Usually…

DANIELLE

Let's not us the word usually anymore today Brent. We've told her that dressing oddly does not make her talented. Jill even advised her once that the zoos were full, and that she needed something more. It clearly didn't register. Did she call herself Kathy or Katy?

BRENT

Katy, I think. Why, is it important?

DANIELLE

No, not really. She oscillates between the two at some random cycle. It's like the disk on a craps table, on and off, seemingly at the toss of the dice. When it's Kathy, she is off men.

BRENT

Off men? Is that a fad?

DANIELLE

No, it's more of a fast than a fad.

BRENT

And when it's Katy?

DANIELLE

When it's Katy, then the all you can eat buffet is open. And Katy likes buffets.

BRENT

Does everyone in your family suffer from nymphomania?

DANIELLE

Not, it's mainly just the women. And even then, it really is just a small percentage.

BRENT

Like 70%?

DANIELLE

Be serious Brent, you're one of the few non family males in attendance. Of course all of the single women are attracted to you.

BRENT

It's not the single women that concern me, Danielle. It's all of these widows with a stringer of dead husbands in their hands. They'd be great at fishing.

DANIELLE

They don't have the patience for that, unless you mean spear fishing.

BRENT

Let's talk about my big interview with Trudy? Should I change into a suit? Ok, I'll be serious.

DANIELLE

Are we serious? Because if we weren't serious, I would not have asked you to attend today.

BRENT

Are we serious? Because if we aren't serious, I wouldn't be here today.

DANIELLE

Even if the Yankees had a bullpen?

BRENT

Even then. So your great aunt Trudy, her approval is a good sign?

DANIELLE

It's essential. Some of my cousins have gone against her, in other words they paid no attention to what she said, or what she said by not saying it.

DANIELLE

I don't understand what you just said.

DANIELLE

Whatever message she sends to you is really meant for me. It's is up to me to understand her message.

BRENT

She just can't send you a private text?

DANIELLE

You mustn't ridicule her method.   Sending me a private text is exactly what she does. She just does her in own way. Consider yourself a carrier pigeon, you don't need to be able to read. If she asks you a question, consider it very carefully before answering.

BRENT

What do I do if the question is written? Remember, us pigeons can't read. You talk like this is a real interview.

DANIELLE

That's what I've been trying to tell you. Yes, this is an interview.

BRENT

Ok, ok. So I listen to the question carefully before responding; that rules out being flippant.

DANIELLE

No, it doesn't. Flippant might be the absolute perfect attitude.

BRENT

One can't be flippant in a considered manner. I'd just look stupid, or slow.

DANIELLE

That won't matter with her, normal rules don't apply in interviews. This interview is no exception.   There are always trick questions that are the real questions.

BRENT

Hmm, I'm not sure that makes sense.

DANIELLE

Ok, pretend that you're speaking to her and she said the same thing to you "Normal rules don't apply in interviews, this one is no exception".   Think for a minute, don't be overly clever, or caustic. How would you respond?

BRENT

Ok, the same way. I'd still say "Hmm, I'm not sure that makes sense".

DANIELLE

Perfect.

BRENT

It is?

DANIELLE

Yes. Or it might be completely wrong.

BRENT

Great.

DANIELLE

The important thing is to be

BRENT

Serious?

DANIELLE

Yes, serious, and to be respectful, but above all honest.

BRENT

Despite all of the strange goings on that I've experienced here at the farm these past few hours, there is a hell of a lot of seriousness in your family, Danielle. You should have just said that at the beginning. You made it sound like I'm playing Russian roulette with a Russian pointing the revolver at me while he, excuse me, she, slowly pulls the trigger.

DANIELLE

Trudy is French, not Russian, but keep in mind that roulette was invented by the French.

A flight attendant told me once that the cockpit of a modern jetliner, I forget which model, has 164 buttons, each with an individual purpose, and that the pilots had to be knowledgeable about of each of them. Trudy knows all of our family's button and the story of each.

BRENT

That way that you've explained it to me, she understands how to push them. Not necessarily when or why, just how.

DANIELLE

I think that she comprehends the when and why as well. We are not as clever as she, and therefore we don't follow her logic. I've learned to give her the benefit of the doubt. But she isn't as young as she once was.

BRENT

To the extent that you now you doubt the benefit?

DANIELLE

I don't know. And now that the moment of your interview is here, I wonder if I am putting too much effort into getting Trudy's approval.

Maybe not getting her approval is actually her approval.

I wish that you hadn't said that. What you suggest might be true

True at false at the same time, only here in Button land.

I'm going to just ignore your mockery and stick with my original plan. I've found what her hottest button is.

BRENT

Yes?

DANIELLE

Guess.

BRENT

I'm not good at guessing. I'm electing to pass on the scavenger hunt for that reason. Just tell me.

DANIELLE

You can't pass on the scavenger hunt. We can talk about that later.

Her button is not having any of her other buttons pushed. She believes that most people are rude, cruel, obnoxious, etc., and if someone is not rude to her at least once it undermines faith in her own bizarre logic. So someone being unfailingly polite and kind and easygoing drives her over the edge.

I've always wanted one of the new attendees behave like that to her. That I'd like to see!

BRENT

I have a growing suspicion that you've finally admitted the real reason for my attendance today at this.......

DANIELLE

Peaceful family reunion?

I was going to say bullfight.   Bullfight in French is what?

DANIELLE

La Corrida

BRENT

Corrida or Roulette. It's nice to have a choice. Yes Cherie, many wonderful things are French. I'm as ready as I ever will be.

DANIELLE

Me too, I have my rabbit's foot in my pocket.

SCENE 4

(*George escorts Trudy to porch from stage left, she sits in rocking chair, George remains standing*).

GEORGE

On the drive in I noticed that the old Meredith farm is gone, it's been transformed into just another subdivision.

TRUDY

Meredith.   How often do you hear that name? The old man used to come and visit us a lifetime ago. Now it is only a street. It used to be a life, many lives, a family, a working farm, children.

GEORGE

In brief, life?

TRUDY

Life, and death. A tombstone has your name, your full name, and dates. Here, an entire family, the Merediths, have vanished, nearly forgotten, only a simple street sign to mark their fleeting existence. Despite the best efforts they are still dead. Cleaning their tombstones every three years doesn't alter the fact that they remain nothing but dust.
No dynasty, nothing.

GEORGE

And for us? No dynasty for the Buttons?

TRUDY

I'm just being cranky. It happens. The word is melancholic?

GEORGE

Yes.

TRUDY

That would be a good name for a cocktail.

GEORGE

It would need to contain Bitters, I think?

TRUDY

Very good. You are ever the wordsmith. Look, near the ridge. There goes Tucker, George.

GEORGE

Who? Oh, Tucker.

TRUDY

Your grandson. Who is that with him? It looks like it could be a girl, but it's hard to tell from this distance.

GEORGE

I don't see anyone else. But then you always did have excellent vision. What did the others call it? X-ray eyes?

TRUDY

X-ray eyes. I haven't heard that expression in years. Oh, they're beyond the ridgeline now. They are gone from sight.

GEORGE

Beyond your X-ray vision?

GEORGE

I wonder where he is off to, there's nothing in that direction.

TRUDY

That's likely the attraction. He has to prove to himself that there really is nothing there. He will be disappointed. He will find something, they always do.

GEORGE

How do you know that Trudy?

TRUDY

Experience, too much experience. Boys always find something, regardless of how hard they try not to.

GEORGE

You're referring to me now, obviously. I was wondering when you would target me. Discussions with you always have undercurrents and hidden meanings.

Let's focus on Tucker.

TRUDY

Focus on Tucker? That would be novel for the writer of novels.

GEORGE

Knowing him, he probably has a map and a compass, but no idea how to use either one, let alone how to use them together.

TRUDY

Do you know Tucker?

GEORGE

Yes, of course. Well, no. (*pause*) Not really. You do realize that Tucker doesn't live with me? He's only here because I asked my daughter if she and Tucker were coming to the Button reunion. She said yes, which meant something near to yes, which finished by meaning only that she had me as an unpaid baby sitter for a few days, and that Tucker would out of the way here at the farm..

TRUDY

I see. I won't ask you what Rita had planned that required Tucker's being out of the way. It doesn't matter in any case.

GEORGE

I didn't pose any questions to Rita myself, for the very same reasons. Her answers never matter even in those rare instances that they make sesnse. Rita and her ex-husband Tyler are like two sports cars that sideswiped each other one night. Neither one either slowed down or stopped, leaving behind them, as the only sign of their collision, a son, Tucker.

TRUDY

Tucker is more than road debris.

GEORGE

That, I do know, Trudy.

TRUDY

I hope so. From the little that I've seen and spoken with Tucker, he seems to be a wonderful child.

GEORGE

He is. But I'm not a wonderful grandfather. And I've written enough twisting mysteries to be suspicious of this whole weekend.

TRUDY

What do you mean by that? You're referring to your daughter?

GEORGE

Yes. Rita is clever enough to see this as a method of making the situation permanent. This situation that I refer to, well, I'm concerned that she wants Tucker to live with me full time. It's probably best for her..

TRUDY

And better for Tucker, but not better for you.   Is that what you were going to say?

GEORGE

Yes, and for you.

TRUDY

Me?

GEORGE

You are too old Trudy, to attempt the little old innocent me look. That gambit doesn't work on family members anyway. I may not have your X-ray eyes, but I have a pretty good nose. And eyesight good enough to spot your phone number on Tucker's cell phone. It lasted too long a time to be a call between a young boy and an old woman.

TRUDY

A young boy and an old woman. Yes, I imagine that is what we are and how you think of us.

GEORGE

I'm sorry.

TRUDY

A young boy and an oldish, uncaring grandfather. How long should one like that be, George?

GEORGE

All I know is that your phone conversation was too long. Period. Did Rita call you from Tucker's phone, since you wouldn't answer a call from hers? I'm right, aren't I, Trudy?

TRUDY

Yes. Tucker is your responsibility. There is no one else. You could live here, with me.

GEORGE

He is his parents' responsibility.

TRUDY

In theory, yes. If he had parents. You're old enough to know that theory means nothing here.

GEORGE

I'm old enough to realize that life, my life -- it really is all about me. Without me, none of this exists. I believe that a man passes through a stage of invisibility twice. Once at age of twelve, where as a boy, he can do anything and get away with it, and again at about round 65 or 70, where the same lack of rules apply. The rest of life is nothing in comparison.
I'm in that second stage. And if this second and final stage burns as quickly as the first, then I have no time for anything, or anyone, but me. I still have a full bucket list.

TRUDY

Sure. That's where you are in your life. If you survive long enough, you'll understand that it's not all about you.

GEORGE

Hopefully I will die early and won't have to suffer another disappointment. You and this scheme will simply disappear like one of a thousand forgotten, bad dreams. You have this enduring drive to run your portion of the world, and everyone connected with it. Even after your departure.

TRUDY

We all have that drive.

GEORGE

No, most of us couldn't care less. We are too self-centered to be concerned about any legacy. You must have noticed how poorly parents raise children.

TRUDY

So parents shouldn't have kids?

GEORGE

And maybe some kids shouldn't have parents.

TRUDY

But Tucker does. You said earlier that Tucker probably has a map and a compass, but no idea how to use either, let alone together.

GEORGE

Did I?

TRUDY

He doesn't know how to use them together. And he isn't carrying them in case he gets lost; he's carrying them because he already is lost. Don't you see that? It doesn't take x-ray vision.

GEORGE

No, but it helps.

TRUDY

Take advantage of mine. By the way, does Rita intend to have another child?

GEORGE

You should have asked her during your call.

TRUDY

I didn't but I suppose that she will.

GEORGE

I never understood this compelling desire for children, the world does not lack for humans.

TRUDY

It's the most natural need in the world. But I agree, we're not short on inventory when it comes to humanity. Nevertheless it's difficult to find good people. It is even more difficult to make them. Genetics is a crapshoot, just look at cousin Harold and his contribution to the human species.

GEORGE

So you see something special in Tucker? Is that it?

TRUDY

I see something special in everyone. More importantly, I see something useful in Tucker. We need useful as much as we need special.

GEORGE

That's very mercenary.

TRUDY

Thank you. It's nice to be recognized as not being a sweet, dotty old woman. Your upgrading of me to a mercenary old women is a compliment.

GEORGE

You are welcome.

TRUDY

That's another trait that we need; toughness.   So, getting back to your mission, you need to treat Tucker as a project. He needs to be number one on your ridiculous bucket list. That movie has done nothing except to make men even more self-centered and childish..   As for helping Tucker, it is beyond clear that you have difficulty in doing this out of love.

People today feel free to say anything they want, just as long as they don't mean it. Everyone gets perpetual do-overs. Life has become a fictional YouTube video, with everyone uploading their own fantasies, replacing those of yesterday's movie stars. Oh, don't look so surprised George, yes, I'm internet literate.

I don't have many friends on the internet, hell, I don't have many friends at all, they're all either dead or wishing that they were. But I meet some of their children and grandchildren. It's rare that I meet one who doesn't suffer from a bad case of social media. Its epidemic.
(*pause*) Where was I?

GEORGE

Trying to direct my life via YouTube, I think. So, what's your point? Escapes from reality have dropped in price, to the point that anyone can afford a pocketful of them.

TRUDY

George, I'll make it easy for you. You've written some very successful books. You need to treat Tucker as the main character in a book, you need to nurture him, and direct him. And in order to do it well, you need to be close to him. You can't recreate him from scratch. He already exists, like a character in a sequel. If you can't do out of love, fake it.

GEORGE

And you suggest that I do it here, that we live here with you?

TRUDY

Yes, you'll need to pay for some remodeling work. You will be able to write it off as some research on childhood development in a rural community, you might even get some grant money. If not, we'll bury it under some farm subsidy. Understand that this will be remodeling for both the house and for Tucker. I'll be here to help, for a while that is. You know about my illness?

GEORGE

Yes, Aunt Jill mentioned it...

TRUDY

This illness hasn't affected my critical thinking skills.

GEORGE

No, you're certainly as critical as always.

TRUDY

Nor does the medication.

GEORGE

No? I thought that Aunt..

TRUDY

It was affecting me, and I didn't like that effect. That's why I stopped taking it.

GEORGE

I am sorry to hear that, Trudy. The pain must be terrible. You love the family that much?

TRUDY

No, not everyone. You for example only rate a 5 or 6 on a scale of ten.

GEORGE

Oh.

TRUDY

Don't pout! Pouting will only lower your score. A six on my scale is decent, I'm a tough judge. I do what I do out of duty. Love is the squishy side of duty. As far as the pain, I learned years ago that you can't experience the pain of another person.

GEORGE

Someone was famous for his "I feel your pain" comment.

TRUDY

Typical BS, you should know better. I pity God, He can't even know death, nonexistence. For Him, there is no oblivion, no escape. And he's burdened us with the same affliction, if you follow that sort of belief.

GEORGE

A billion Christians might take exception with your interpretation of their religion.

TRUDY

Eternity must be such a bore. I don't see the attraction of it. What pleasure is there in being immortal?

GEORGE

You're only human, you're limited.

TRUDY

Au contraire, I'm not limited, according to you. I have no permanent off switch, I'm like the mechanical rabbit in those commercials; I'm not offered the choice of declining another battery. I'm forced to go on and on and on. I'd like to blast that damned bunny with a 12 gauge at least once.

GEORGE

Well, you and I could spend time together in eternity, Trudy, like we're doing here.

TRUDY

Oh sure, we could hang out together in eternity. That might be fun for an hour or so, maybe even a few days, even the time it takes to launch project Tucker. Then what? No thanks George. You're only a six here on Earth. Your rating would drop dramatically on the other side.

GEORGE

Alright, Trudy, I am willing to hear details on this new living arrangement.
Do you have any suggestions for me? Interviewing a 12 year old boy can be
intimidating; it's like first contact with an alien life form. We don't even
share the same cultural reference points; if I try to be "cool", I'll feel foolish,
like an inept spy who is simply sent home by the enemy out of pity. Even
our language is different.

TRUDY

Think of it as learning a foreign language together. By the way he should be
learning French. You too.

GEORGE

At my age? It has been a long time since I spoke French.

TRUDY

If French doesn't work for you, then when you are together, simply pretend
that you are speaking to a younger version of yourself.

GEORGE

I'm not sure that there ever was a younger version of me.

TRUDY

You can reread your own journals from that age.

GEORGE

I burned them. It was their time.

TRUDY

Oh? Good. They were crap anyway.

GEORGE

You read them? How could you?

TRUDY

I couldn't. I tried, but as I said, they were crap. I wanted to burn them myself. Your wife leaving you was the best thing that ever happened to you. People don't change that much, not even you.

GEORGE

Is that a compliment or an insult?

TRUDY

Neither. All you have to do, is to imagine that you have no worries: no money concerns, no serious romances, either past, present, or future, no real job either.

GEORGE

So I have no romance, no job, and no money?

TRUDY

Yes

GEORGE

This might be easier than I thought. I remember it well, being three for three in those categories.

TRUDY

With a bright, but imaginary future in front of you. Ask him about his writing or what he thinks about writing. Just ask him questions.

GEORGE

Trudy, if you were me, you'd have no compunction about doing this?

TRUDY

I'm mercenary, you said so yourself. I never have any compunction. For me it's on permanent backorder.

GEORGE

No compunction about lying to your own children?

TRUDY

No.

GEORGE

Just no?

TRUDY

Tucker is your grandson, not your son. Lying to him should be even easier. I wanted to keep it simple for you. That's all that we do, lie. As soon as children can read, we present them with these horrid fairy tales, filled with talking bears and magical unicorns. Why do we this to them?

GEORGE

I don't know, but surely you do. You've seen it with your X-ray eyes.

TRUDY

Very good. Yes, we do this to prepare them for bigger and bigger lies. A few children eventually learn to recognize and reject lies, but not to reject the values of lies.

GEORGE

Lies can be helpful in the right proportion?

TRUDY

Obviously.

Unfortunately most children learn instead to accept lies. I really can't envision a worse way to raise children. In our efforts to inoculate the majority against falsehoods, we fail terribly and end by indoctrinating them with fantasies.

GEORGE

Our vaccinations bring on the very illness it is intended to prevent?

TRUDY

In the majority of cases, yes. I can't be more clear.

GEORGE

Any here you are, advising me to perpetuate this brain washing. You put yourself in charge. I evidently missed the election

TRUDY

Democracy is overrated. Now you understand. Good.

GEORGE

No, not really. But I'm willing to go along with your machinations, if only to see where they end.

TRUDY

 Now that I have you back on the right path, I need to mingle with the family, give my seated tour of the farm highlights, past and present, and of course do my interviews.

GEORGE

Danielle's beau, Brent?

TRUDY

Yes, among others.

GEORGE

He seems ok.

TRUDY

We'll see.

GEORGE

You mean that you'll see, with your X-ray eyes.

TRUDY

It's not magic, George, most people could do what I do.

GEORGE

I doubt that very much.

TRUDY

It's a chore, there are always plenty of those.

GEORGE

In running the farm?

TRUDY

Yes, but also in managing a family.

GEORGE

And yourself? Your…

TRUDY

As far as I know, my health today is fine.

GEORGE

And tomorrow, and the day after?

TRUDY

Every day is a gift, so they say. Life is not something that you regift. It is more like a Christmas tree; everyone adds something to it. I'm fine, George. Would I lie?

SCENE 5

DANIELLE

Trudy, Jill told me to let you know that something is missing from the nightstand in your bedroom upstairs. And who is the Morgan? No one seems to know.

TRUDY

There are over 150 attendees here, many of them are debutants. I don't know all of them myself, not yet.

DANIELLE

163 at last count, according the sheet at the sign-in tent. I've spoken to many of the parents..

TRUDY

I wouldn't worry about it. Did Jill mention what she thought was missing. If it's my medication, then good. I'd hoped that if I ignored the pill bottle long enough, that it would take the hint and go looking for another, more receptive patient.

DANIELLE

No, it's not your medicine, its *(leans down to whisper in Trudy's ear)*.

SCENE 1

TRUDY

Danielle, what is the matter? And why are you whispering?

DANIELLE

Jill said that your revolver is missing from the upstairs bedroom.

TRUDY

Jill said that my revolver is missing! (*pretends to panic*). It must have been Tucker. Let's keep this just between us for the moment. There is no need to alarm the men. They would only to struggle to come up with a plan and an organization chart. By that time, we'll be done. Where is George?

TRACIE

He is down in the lower field, watching badminton and speaking with Jill.

TRUDY

Perfect, at least that is on track. We now need to find Tucker. I'll need my hiking boots.

TRACIE

You have hiking boots? Will they even fit? You're not in any shape..

TRUDY

Of course the boots will fit. I haven't let myself go, have I? I walk a mile every day.

My boots are in the attic. Tracie, you can climb those steps easier than I can. And the light isn't very good up there anyway. Watch your steps at you mount the stairs, they're not very even, and the attic floorboard aren't level or nailed down in some spots. (*Tracie exits*)

But first, Danielle, fetch my bottle of joint juice from the fridge, it's the nasty green looking stuff. I'll dose myself with a double shot for this expedition. And, oh yes, one more thing, grab a fresh pack of cigarettes from the sugar canister. Do you have all that? Good.
Finally, we'll bring that topographic map, hanging in the parlor.

DANIELLE

That map is gone. I noticed its absence before I came to notify you. They must have taken it with them.

TRUDY

They? Who are they?

DANIELLE

Tucker and this mysterious Morgan.

TRUDY

Have you seen this Morgan?

DANIELLE

I don't know, there are a lot of kids here. I guess I could have. I'm not even sure if this Morgan is a boy or a girl.

TRUDY

There are a dozen or more girls here at the reunion, it could have been any of them, or none of them. Tucker is still young enough to treat girls as equal humans. I don't recall hearing of any males with that name in the family.

DANIELLE

In fact, when Tucker mentioned the name, I thought it might be a made up friend, he said that he was going to hike to Morgan's rock with this Morgan. We all thought that it was funny at the time. But now, with the missing item... Well, let me get you your things from the kitchen. (*Danielle exits stage right. Trudy sits there quietly, looking into the distance, chuckles once and then is quiet until Danielle quickly returns with green juice and an unopened pack of cigarettes. Trudy laughs*)

DANIELLE

What's so funny?

TRUDY

You are. (*sets juice aside and fills cup with wine from a bottle found on the porch next to her, and takes a sip*). This wine tastes about the same as this horrid green stuff, but it is free, courtesy of Uncle Bert. It works about the same, I suppose. (*pause*) First, no one is going anywhere. You're panicking at the drop of a hat. Tucker went for a walk, by himself or maybe with a cousin. Why are you worrying?

DANIELLE

But he has been gone for hours.

TRUDY

He'll be fine. He has a compass, and a map.

(*Tracie returns carrying tall dusty boots, a broad brimmed hat, and a whistle*)

DANIELLE

You're extremely creative in finding ways to block out any thoughts of your grandnephew, who at this very moment may be fighting off a rabid bear with the dead body of a rattlesnake that had just bit him.

TRUDY

He always did like animals.

TRACIE

Maybe not a rabid bear, but then, who would like one of those?

DANIELLE

Did? You talk about him in the past tense. You sound like George writing his next book where another family member suffers a gruesome death. Do you see us only as characters to be manipulated by you?

(*Trudy dusts off, inspects, and slowly begins donning boots and hat, strings whistle around her neck*)

Look at George, oblivious to everything. And if anything goes horribly wrong with Tucker, George will be able to come up with some not so heartfelt words.

TRACIE

Let's not over react. The farm has always been a safe place.

TRUDY

I remember these boots, it's been years since I've used them as intended. I hiked and rock climbed in these wooded mountains, alone. Tucker will be fine. Women back then had ambitions and role models, they simply lacked the array of opportunities that everyone, girls included, enjoy today. They still do. But that doesn't eliminate boys, they have ambition and role models as well.

DANIELLE

Does George even know Tucker's middle name..

TRUDY

There are meat hooks in the barn, along with hooks for hay, pitchforks, axes, hatchets, and some nasty looking tools for doing who knows what. Not to mention chainsaws, bailers, reciprocating blade devices that would slice through a bone as if it were a cornstalk. And never was there not a dog in residence, I remember one who spent afternoons mastering his snarl. He did very well, considering that he had no access to a mirror.

DANIELLE

His birthday...

TRUDY

Of course, whenever there was any time of a bruise or cut, the victim's siblings always overreacted. Amputation was always the first option.

DANIELLE

..the last four digits of his social security number.

TRUDY

Ask him that tomorrow. He'll know all of those answers tomorrow.

DANIELLE

Why, what is so special about tomorrow? (*splash offstage*) See, anything can happen to a child here? That boy just took a dunk in the pond, right in front of a dozen adults. He must be about the same age as Tucker.

TRUDY

Was it one of odd Harold's kids?

TRACIE

I think so, but it's pretty hard to tell with all the mud and lily pad leaves on him.

TRUDY

I figured as much. It's probably his first bath in weeks. I'd wager that even coated in fermented pond muck, he smells better now than when he arrived.

Danielle, ask him those questions and any others that you might have. But ask them tomorrow. Today, let George be George. And let Tucker be Tucker. Tucker needs some private time. He needs time to be a boy, to have boy adventures. It not against the law. It may not be what you want, but it is what he needs. Just as I may not enjoy living in this electronic, www 21st century world, but I accept that it is not illegal to drink and internet.

TRACIE

But it is illegal, isn't it, for a twelve year old boy to be walking around with a revolver. And even if it were legal, it's not safe.

TRUDY

Any parents who don't raise children to be safe around weapons by the time they are twelve, probably shouldn't have weapons themselves.

DANIELLE

This is not the time for political discussions. We all know that Tucker doesn't have real parents.   And many of the children here younger than twelve. Tracie, are you coming along?

TRUDY

Which is why I locked all the firearms in the trunk of my car. I must not have told Jill, but she should be well aware of that already. I do it every reunion.

TRACIE

Great. I knew that you had things under control, Trudy, you always do. So, I guess the crisis is averted. I have one question that I'd like to ask today. (*Trudy nods*) Since you knew all this, why did you put your boots and hat on?

TRUDY

Someone told me recently that twelve was the best age for a boy. With the boots and hat, I wanted to relive my best age.

DANIELLE

I'm going to search for Tucker, even though he is not my grandson.
.

TRUDY

Children need to not need us sometime. Today is as good as any for Tucker. Here he can solo better than anywhere else.

TRACIE

Are you ok Trudy? What are you drinking? Uncle Bert's wine?

TRUDY

Alcohol doesn't make you an adult, it emulates the infirmities of old age. Stumbling, memory loss, slurred speech. The hangover is a taste of daily life in the horrendous future that awaits you. Being old is like being a combination of being drunk in the body and hungover in the head. I don't recommend it.

DANIELLE

Trudy?

TRUDY

Oh, Danielle, I'm fine. It's about time that I enjoyed myself at one of these reunions. This is my first and only glass of wine. It really is terrible. It lacks everything that makes for a wine, let alone a good wine. It is just bad. Still it's better than the alternative (*indicating juice*)

DANIELLE

I'm leaving now.

TRUDY

Look, way over there, isn't that Tucker. He reappeared from the other side of the ridge a few minutes ago. You girls don't handle teasing very well. It's still early.

TRACIE

Let's go meet him.

TRUDY

No, he needs to complete this trip by himself. He'll be here in 15 or 20 minutes. That gives me time to enjoy this glass of alleged wine and to tell my story.

You mentioned the name Morgan earlier, Danielle? Tucker was going to hike to Morgan's Rock, with Morgan? (*Danielle nods*)

TRACIE

I heard him say it too. You know sometimes kids can be little smart…

TRUDY

Yes. Big kids too.

DANIELLE

But there doesn't seem to be a Morgan here. So I assumed that Tucker was either just teasing us, you're right, we don't handle it well, or else he was just pretending. He's still young enough for that sort of thing.

TRUDY

Is George still speaking with Jill, oh yes, I see him now. And who is that with them, Anna Riswell?

TRACIE

Yes, it's Anna. She never looks a day older. At this distance, it's hard to determine age, but I was speaking with her earlier and she hasn't aged at all.

TRACIE

She didn't bring her creepy daughter I hope that would ruin everything.

DANIELLE

Ruin everything how?

TRACIE

No, Laura had to work today. No rest for the wicked as they say.

TRUDY

Never more true than in her case.

DANIELLE

I don't know Laura do I?

TRUDY

Consider yourself lucky, Danielle.   Laura is the local mortician, very successful and talented from what I hear. She is just creepy, always has been and still is.

DANIELLE

The soil here is excellent for raising creepy.

TRUDY

Laura is younger than her mother Anna of course, but you'd swear that they are the same age. Laura's heavy self-application of makeup from mortician's kit doesn't help. And her kids.

TRACIE

She has a few kids, more than a few, really, a regular herd.

TRUDY

I can't keep track of them. She pops them out like clockwork. I wouldn't be shocked to hear that she only has them as a supply of spare parts for her old age.

DANIELLE

She can't be as bad as you describe, Trudy. You're painting her as a real ghoul.

TRUDY

Ghoul? That is exactly the word that fits Laura. She's definitely not the type that I'd go camping with alone. And if it was Laura instead of Morgan who accompanied Tucker on his hike, I'd have given him the revolver, with at least one reload of ammunition, and a wooden stake to boot. (*pause*) Morgan's Rock. We used to have a Morgan in the family. That was her middle name. We all knew here as Lydia.

DANIELLE

Really? Your sister Lydia?

TRUDY

Yes, my sister sometimes referred to herself as Morgan, when she was doing something adventurous.

DANIELLE

Does everyone in our family have two names?   What is up with that?

TRUDY

Even these boots belonged to her. She left them behind for me when she went into the worlds. I'm sure she found replacements elsewhere.

TRACIE

I've not heard of Lydia/Morgan before, neither from you or anyone else. How then did Tucker?

TRUDY

You must have forgotten. No one has a monopoly on imagination. At least Tucker seems to bring his women to life, unlike his grandfather, who just whacks them left and right. See girls, nothing bad has happened here today.

DANIELLE

You're tempting fate with that kind of talk, Trudy.

TRUDY

Don't worry about Fate, my dear. He's a cousin too.

SCENE 2

JILL

I'm so pleased that you had a chance to speak with Anna.

GEORGE

She and you are really lifelong friends. She seemed…

JILL

So much younger than her age. Don't worry. I hear that all the time. Or, oh, Anna can't be that old. That is another line. Folks phrase it that way instead of blurting out what they actually think.   Like, she appears so much younger than you Jill, or Anna can't be as old as you.

GEORGE

Would you feel better if I told you that I was going to say that she seemed as vivacious as you?

JILL

Were you?

GEORGE

No. (*Jill smacks George on the arm*). But I will. It's true. You and she are both lively even though see looks much younger. (*another smack*) Anna is a widow for how long now?

JILL

Let me think, it was around the holidays. That would be about 18 months now. She woke up morning and Henry had died during the night.

GEORGE

That is the best way, to pass quietly while sound asleep, instead of suffering from a long, drawn out illness. Henry was fortunate.

JILL

So was Anna. For her it was only one day with a cold, *unresponsive husband. Mine was cold and unresponsive for 23 years. (pause)* It's funny, now that I think of it.

GEORGE

What's funny?

JILL

I'm just thinking about Anna and Henry. They were about the same age, Henry was only a year ahead of us in school, but three years older. Schools used to flunk kids back then.

GEORGE

I remember, when we were kids, Flunk was the only F word we knew.

JILL

Schools mess up in not holding students back anymore; six years of high school is much cheaper than a college degree for maturing a young person. It's like following a recipe, sometimes your oven is just not that hot and you need to bake the muffins a little bit longer.

But that isn't what struck me as being funny. It wasn't their age difference, it was despite the fact that although Henry and Anna were only three years apart, he looked so much older.

GEORGE

We just discussed her youthful appearance. Anna looks much younger than her contemporaries. So?

JILL

Yeah, I know. But in their house they had this photograph of themselves, taken on a Caribbean cruise several years ago. He told me that he'd bought two copies, one for himself and Anna, and one for their daughter, Laura.

GEORGE

Isn't the daughter a little weird?

JILL

Yeah, a bit. We can discuss her next. You didn't visit us last year, so you will just need to wait and take the latest news at the pace I deliver it. You can't fast forward me like some DVR. So, in this photo, Henry didn't have any wrinkles, not a one. He looked younger than the day before he was born. It was like something out of a wax museum. He was so proud of it. He and Anna looked to be the same age, finally.

GEORGE

He had plastic surgery during the cruise?

JILL

No. Not at all. How on Earth did you come up with that conclusion? The photo was just touched up with an airbrush by the photographer on the ship. Anna displayed the photograph at the funeral home, she may have even put it in the casket with him. People do that these days, put things in with the deceased. I don't understand it, those coffins don't have shelves, or even a fold down tray, and it's not like Henry was King Tut. Are you following me, George?

GEORGE

I'm still in the same zip code as you, but I may be falling behind.

JILL

Henry is in the coffin, the photograph is next to him, and I realized that his daughter Laura, she is a mortician you know, had made up Henry to look exactly like the photograph, down to him wearing the same suit. It was like a commercial or a late night TV testimonial; see how lifelike this customer appears. You can too. The only thing missing was an 800 number. But to those of us who knew him, the late Henry didn't resemble the real Henry at all, but was like

GEORGE

Like an exhibit in a wax museum?

JILL

Yes, that is exactly what it was like. He just duplicated the photograph so perfectly. Of course, he was horizontal instead of vertical, but if you tilted your head just a bit you could almost imagine hearing waves gently slapping the casket like a small Carnival Cruise lifeboat. It was beautiful.

GEORGE

Your own James has been gone about 3 years, hasn't he? Do you think that you are going to remain single?

JILL

I hope not. That's where you come in. Are you?

GEORGE

What, remain single? We're cousins, Jill. The state recently outlawed marriage between cousins.

                              JILL

That is another ridiculous deduction, George. Your leaps of imagination might help you in writing, but not in real life. I'm referring to Anna. Let me tell you more about her. Your probably don't know that she has taken to spending her weekends over in Rose Hill.

                             GEORGE

The psychic village? I visited Rose Hill once in doing some research for a play. It is an interesting place.

                              JILL

Yep. Who knows how much of Henry's money she has wasted trying to contact him on the other side.

                             GEORGE

She must still be grieving. It's only been...

                              JILL

Long enough. It's time to focus on the living. Henry didn't merit a long period of mourning.

                             GEORGE

That's cold, cousin.

                              JILL

So is Henry, dear cousin. We both know that he was never hot stuff.

GEORGE

I never met the man. Maybe he was to Anna.

JILL

Yeah, that is possible. Believe what you want to. Me, I have my own theory.

GEORGE

It must be a doozy of a theory. You've become cynical over the past decade.

JILL

Cynical?

GEORGE

It becomes you. It's as if cynicism is a highlight tint that goes well with your natural color. So, what lead are you pursuing in the Anna Riswell affair?

JILL

Consider this. Anna is not the most spiritual of people. I bet she goes to church every week because she lives in a small town, the same way you set out the garbage bin every week in your subdivision; it's a good way to meet neighbors and it avoids raising a stink.

GEORGE

You have a low opinion of church.

JILL

It's mutual. They see me a sheep, they call me that to my face, and I understand that they want to fleece me on a regular basis. They lied to me so often that I remember their fairy tales, even though I tried to forget them. I was exposed to those twice weekly, for years. If it had been x-rays, I'd be long since dead.

GEORGE

Come on, exposure to religion is not that bad.

JILL

It may not be exactly the same as radiation, but if I were you, I'd blame for them for your hair loss.

GEORGE

We seem to be leaving Anna out of this conversation.

JILL

You're right. Hop! Off she goes to Rose Hill, spraying money on something that she has no faith in, attempting to contact her late, mediocre at best husband, who if he did respond, would scream at her to stop spending his money frivolously.

GEORGE

You have a point, I guess. So what is she doing over there in quaint, quiet Rose Hill?

JILL

The same thing any self-respecting widow would be doing; looking for a replacement.

GEORGE

A replacement husband?

JILL

Ideally, it would be an upgrade, and not just a replacement.

GEORGE

Visiting Rose Hill doesn't necessarily entail spending money. Anna could simply plant herself on a bench there. That would not cost her a dime.

JILL

She has to pay their cover charge. That can add up.

GEORGE

Are investments in husband hunting tax deductible? Why don't you tag along with her if you are so curious?

JILL

Two widows together would frighten away any prospect. It's better to hunt alone. Of course the supply and demand ratio is not to her advantage, and she has to beware of widowers who have the same plan that she does.

GEORGE

Which is for the widower to marry a decent, well off number two widow?

JILL

Or number three or four. Some folks, men included, can be devious.
Nevertheless, Rose Hill is a good fishing hole. What do the young people
call it? IRL. In real life.

GEORGE

In brief, you believe that Anna is pouring money into the hands of psychics
in order for them to help her find luxury class husband number two. Is that
is? Has Anna confirmed this?

JILL

Not really. She doesn't actually need to consult any psychics, she can just
make up her own message from beyond and tailor it to each man she meets.
Fortunately, she still has an excellent memory and won't mix up her

GEORGE

Lies? She won't mix up her lies to each man?

JILL

Lines, not lies, her numerous fishing lines.

GEORGE

You call them lines, I call the lies. I get the picture; you and Anna both want
new husbands.

JILL

It's as simple as hello.

GEORGE

Tell me the bad news. What are Anna's faults, her cons versus her pros?

JILL

Personal cons? None.

GEORGE

None?

JILL

No major ones.

GEORGE

And as to her not so personal major faults?

JILL

Laura.

GEORGE

The weird daughter (*Jill nods yes*)

JILL

Actually, you she does remind me of you in a way.

GEORGE

In being a major fault, or in being weird?

JILL

You write books, Laura has children. You each produce one at about the same rate.

GEORGE

There is nothing wrong with having children.

JILL

You wouldn't have said that an hour ago. Your books are, well, not good. Your invented characters are terrible; so are her creations. I'm sorry George, but I'm as entitled to an opinion as much as anyone else.

GEORGE

I've enough critics outside of the family.

JILL

The most effective ones are those who share your genes. Your books are popular, just not with me. At least I can throw them away or burn them. Her kids, I don't know about whether she gets rid of one now and again or not. She has about the same number as the last time I saw her.

And, like yours, her marriage was a predictable waste of time, although I did miss the over/under on it.

GEORGE

The over and under? As in betting? On whose, mine or hers?

JILL

Hers. I was right on with your marriage. Your breakup was a jackpot.

GEORGE

It's so comforting to have family support.

JILL

Aside from Laura, and her baggage train of young delinquents, Anna is quite the catch.

GEORGE

Earlier, you described Anna as a fisherman, now she is the catch of the day. Let me ask you, why hasn't she either landed a man or been landed by one? She has plenty of opportunity. Is the daughter that big of an anchor?

JILL

I think that Anna wants more than what that particular lake has to offer. She wants an upgrade, someone who

GEORGE

Someone who writes very successful, not very good books, filled with terrible characters?

JILL

I thought that you had a thicker skin.   The fact is, my best friend is hoarding all of the decent eligible men. If they want to contact dead wives then they're faithful unto death. I like that, a lot. I find that quality appealing, more than Anna does. Faithfulness is more attractive than some photo shopped image on Timber.

GEORGE

I think you mean Tinder.

JILL

Not in this neck of the woods, we're in the middle of Pennsylvania, believe me the site we use, er, that folks use, is a local one called Timber.   It has certainly brought about a revival at the town library. I'm not the only one without home internet.

GEORGE

I can only imagine steamy library book aisles serving as the site of middle aged hookups. Have you been on real dates?

JILL

A few.

GEORGE

You should be careful.

JILL

Careful? Everything that I want to do is dangerous. Even this sunblock, oops, it only claims to be a sunscreen now, has side effects. I may as well just sit here, but, no, sitting is the new smoking. These doctors can be such nags; they probably get kickbacks on everything. I'm expecting to be prescribed some gym membership the next time I see my local.   A prescription to Gold's gym.

GEORGE

You mean subscription?

JILL

Whatever. Anna has more opportunity than I do.   Just as you said.

GEORGE

Only because she has decided to overtake you in vivacity.

JILL

Is that really a word? Or are you just too polite to call her a cougar? If you lived her, you could take Anna off the market. You wouldn't have to marry her.

GEORGE

That's nice to hear. I like having a choice.

JILL

Just distract her away from Rose Hill long enough for me to find a husband.

GEORGE

You'd do this to your lifelong friend?

JILL

Do you really enjoy asking foolish questions? We've competed our entire lives, she'd know what I'd be doing. She is likely already weighing the pros and cons of you versus the troop of actual widowers over in physic paradise.

GEORGE

Is an imaginary murdered wife considered a positive or a negative? What is your opinion?

JILL

My opinion doesn't matter, only Anna's does. For what it's worth, I'd say that your novelty is valuable.

GEORGE

Are you sure that it is my novelty and not my novels?

JILL

You are not just another grieving widower, authentic or otherwise.

GEORGE

So many changes are hitting me today, like a basket of bills arriving after Christmas. Lydia's passing was another candle extinguished. Trudy want something from me, something more that is. And now you introduce me to Anna. I'm not saying no to either Trudy or to Anna, it is just a bit overwhelming

I remember being at the farm as a young boy. It was the sight of many of my best memories. Looking back, childhood was peace and adulthood was war, war for the sake of war. Today, I find myself with a twelve year old and no place for me, and with an adult ex-son-in-law who makes of war a career. What happened to us? Peace was a better game.

JILL

You can hope.

GEORGE

We wrap hope in our lives, like hiding medicine in chocolate. But the medicine is nothing more than a placebo. It's all make believe. We humans love to play make believe, the majority of our time dreaming or daydreaming. Which is more real? Sartre said that there was no reality.

JILL

George, if you are going to go all wobbly on me and start gibbering like Shakespeare's Hamlet, I am going to kick you in your codpiece. You still want to be a 12 year old boy. I'm sorry you are just too damn old. That role has been given to Tucker, and while your lines in this play called life are not nearly as dramatic as the stuff you write, it is important. I'm not sure who was a bigger drama queen, George, you or your ex-wife.

I simply suggest that you and Anna have a cup of coffee together sometime, and you have a nervous breakdown. If I'd suggested that you two share a martini, you would have needed a life flight out of here.

Do you fear that Trudy is prying her way into your life, encouraging you to take on Tucker?

GEORGE

Believe it or not, it is even more diabolical, even for Trudy.

JILL

She means well.

GEORGE

She wants me to force myself into Tucker's life. This is a strange, Trudy version of pay it forward. But in this case, I'm stuck with the bill.

You know as well as anyone that a life only has room for one person, it's a small bed that is cramped even with a lover or a spouse. There is no space for even a short term guest such as a grandchild.

JILL

That is the type of garbage that screws up your books, George. It sounds witty, but it simply isn't true. You believe in nothing. Believing nothing is hard work, too much for me, for sure.

It's easier to believe in anything than it is believing in nothing. Don't bother answering. Soon, Tucker won't let any part of you ride along, cluttering up his life, attached to him like a barnacle. You are the parasite, not him. Life confuses us with misdirections, just like your

GEORGE

Second rate stories?

JILL

Tucker is enough like you to reject your best efforts to share his moments. (*pause*) I half read one of your books. There was some James Bond, man about town like character in it. Was he supposed to be you? No? Good. That character had no children, only orphans that he'd dropped unknowingly along his amazing golden highway of a life. You have been cruising along your own autobahn, George.

GEORGE

Tucker's father knows of his existence. He chooses to ignore it. My daughter, too. I used to think that only native Californians could be this self-centered. It has become a national characteristic. I guess that state still sets the trends.

JILL

And you are not self-centered?

GEORGE

Tucker knows that he has been willingly abandoned. And now, I'm expected to assume all responsibility. My daughter said as much, comparing me to some literary villain. Her degree in English literature never got her a job, but it sure helps her to insult me in style.

JILL

Yes, play time is over.   It's time for chores.

GEORGE

Brent told me that his father had no children either. He's turned out ok.

JILL

He had a mother. There is more to existence than you.

GEORGE

Thanks. You don't see it, do you? We are all of us cartoons, it's only a question of who illustrates us. I've chosen to be the cartoonist of my silly, little strip. Although Trudy has halfway convinced me otherwise. I expect Trudy to behave as child, she needs to get her own way.   She criticizes me for doing likewise.

JILL

But her own way results in helping others and not herself.

GEORGE

She isn't a child, but neither is she an adult.

JILL

I've heard that before.

GEORGE

How much longer are you going to continue with this sermon? Your keen insights are beginning to overflow the limited capacity of my dark soul. Listen, I know all this about me. You are not the first and certainly not the most articulate chronicler of my shortcomings. My shortcomings are lengthy, according to most experts, present company included.

JILL

I'm sorry if I offended you.

GEORGE

When I hear "I'm sorry that I've offended you", I know that the barrage of insults is only halfway over. You can save the rest of your rockets for someone else. One fireworks show is much like another. Hell, you're not even angry with me.

JILL

You visited the farm as a young boy, George. But your times here were only and always during the summer. You missed the bleakness of winter. Are you leaving right after the reunion? Off to Rome, or Hawaii, or, have you thought about visiting cousin Doug in Paris?

GEORGE

I don't know, my schedule may change. Are you jealous?

JILL

Once, I was very jealous.

GEORGE

I spoke to a cabbie in Malta, who told me that jealousy was among the most popular sports on the island because it was both free and constantly available. I guess that no commercials and no experience needed were pluses as well. Jealousy offers cost without benefit. It's a drug that gives the illusion of pleasure but leaves behind nothing of value.

JILL

Is that the wisdom of your Maltese cab driver, or your own personal experience? I'm jealous of your freedom, but it might just be another illusion. Maybe you can have the chauffeur from Malta weigh in.

Your freedom lets you live like a migratory bird. The short days of Spring and Fall serve you as seasonal runways. You leave us behind, preserved in some amber tinged nostalgia until you decide we again merit your presence. You put us on hold, like those living nativity sets captured on stage, but in your mind, that is ok, because we inhabit some beautiful, eternal summer.

GEORGE

You exaggerate. Sure I come here in the summer, but endless summer? I wish. If I were rich...

JILL

You are!

GEORGE

I'm not.

JILL

You may not be your rich but believe me you are absolutely my rich. If I were my rich, perhaps I'd be like you. I too would follow the geese, and the ducks, and even those tiny hummingbirds with their minuscule brains, but all wise enough to winter in summer.

GEORGE

That would make for a wonderful movie title.

JILL

Winter in summer. You should write that. Try to make it less not so good.

GEORGE

There is more to a book, or a movie, than simply a title. Not much more, perhaps, but some It's not as if I take blank pages and sprinkle some special water on them and the stories magically appear in some previously hidden ink. It is work. The characters become real to me.

JILL

And after these characters of yours become real, you have them permanently pasted into books and put on a shelf. They are forgotten.

GEORGE

Well, you could put it that way, I suppose.   But sometimes I bring them back.

JILL

Yes, like your murdered wife. You take them down from the shelf, when you need them, or you have an urge to live the moment again.   Are we all characters?

GEORGE

Or sometimes

JILL

Or sometimes just to sell a new story?

GEORGE

It is my work, Jill.

JILL

So you say.

GEORGE

They aren't real. Even Sophie wasn't Shannon. Sophie wasn't real.

JILL

Yes, she was.

GEORGE

Are you sure?

JILL

Yes. I can still distinguish between flesh and fantasy. Take Tucker for instance.

GEORGE

Take Tucker. That is the order of the day. Trudy and Rita press me to take him for much longer. You too?

JILL

You're putting him on a shelf without letting him live. He's not some character in one your books.

GEORGE

Remnants.

JILL

What remnants?

GEORGE

That is what I call them, remnants. Characters who are and remain undeveloped ideas, they don't even make it to the shelf. They end up in a file labeled remnant characters. Trudy suggested that I should treat him as a character in a new book

JILL

I don't believe that. You must have misunderstood. You know that she can talk in riddles like some rural oracle. It can be wearisome. And with her illness.

GEORGE

She said that treating him as a character, I think she used the term project, would help me to get to know him. She told me that I have a duty to, oh I don't know, be a grandfather.

JILL

That sounds better. She usually knows what she is talking about. She's still sharp. She and I are saying the same thing,

GEORGE

Yes, almost as if you two have rehearsed it. (*pause*)

The past was an idyllic world only because I was a poor observer. To children everything is a game. Adults had jobs, and we kids had toys. I thought of adults as big kids, who complained about their jobs because these toys of theirs were super neat, and complains would prevent us from asking to borrow them.

I'm being childlike, again. It's another character flaw. We're doing well today in cataloging them.

JILL

Provide that same sense of childhood to Tucker. Let him enjoy his real moment, of what, his age of twelve (*nods*), instead of trying to relive yours. Writers are voyeurs. Be one again, for Tucker.

GEORGE

It's easier to build an imaginary world than it is to inhabit your reality.

JILL

Jetting here and there, Rome, walks across Paris,

GEORGE

All of the best places are walkable.

JILL

Like the farm is. Tucker went for a walk today.

GEORGE

Simply being walkable does not promote a place among the best.

JILL

It is a start. And to start something, you need to end something first. The distant book signings, exotic travel research, movie consultations. You've told me all of that. And I'm not jealous, well, maybe a lot jealous. Your best success originated here and your only flesh and blood legacy is here. All this stuff that you've done, and continue to do; don't you find it repetitive?

GEORGE

Why do you accumulate all of this junk? I've seen the attic, and the Jill section in the barn. Since when can cows wear clothes?

JILL

It's not junk. The family accuse me of filling the attic with memorabilia, you're doing the same but it's a solitary attic. They belittle my efforts, saying that some future distant relative or total stranger will simply toss everything into the garbage. Or worse, our photos will end up as a decorative item on the wall of a Cracker Barrel type restaurant, where our images will be laughed at seven days a week over fried chicken and cheese grits.

GEORGE

Perhaps the restaurant will decide to close on Sundays.

JILL

Consider it as a glimpse of the Christmas to come. What possible goal can you have, that you haven't yet accomplished?   You possess no special life lesson to impart to others

GEORGE

Of course not. I'd thank you for bursting my self delusional bubble, but that imploded on its own, decades ago.

JILL

But you do when it comes to Tucker.

GEORGE

Your mother and you have discussed this thoroughly.

JILL

We've been through a few drafts.

GEORGE

I think that this is the command performance, today. Act one, Trudy moves into this house.

JILL

No one really ever moves out of the Button house. What did Brent say? The house is the Button heart.

GEORGE

He'd make a good poet, if the world still appreciated poetry. And then, maybe there would be Tucker and me.

JILL

I hope that that is a yes type maybe.

GEORGE

Maybe.

JILL

Yes.

GEORGE

Now we are in act two. You intend to reel in a big fish from Rose Hill. But you need me to act as a decoy. It doesn't take a psychic, either here or one from Rose Hill, to see that this house would be too small for so many adults.

JILL

We already have a request out to the architect for a proposal.

GEORGE

What does that mean, Jill?

JILL

Well, with my style, and a tiny portion of your immense fortune, we could remodel the house. You would have your own writing desk,

GEORGE

That is extremely generous, Jill. But I'd need an entire room, like I have now in my own house.

JILL

Of course, a wonderful writing room. And I'd finally be able to one up Cousin Joyce.

JILL

Why did you never remarry?

GEORGE

This will sound horrible.

JILL

Truth and honesty often are.

GEORGE

Well, Shannon...

JILL

Sophie?

GEORGE

Honestly, I can't recall. Characters can be more memorable than actual people. Everyone wants to change me. It never ends. Writing is my revenge. They can forget what I said, but they can't ignore what I write. She exhausted me on the idea of marriage. Instead of, pre-marriage classes, they should offer divorce training. Something like, divorce and how to cure it. Anyway, after the breakup, I found myself with enough money to find professional help in raising my daughter.

JILL

But that failed miserably. It's easy to criticize single mothers, but I sometimes think that it improves the child's odds. Single fathers are seen as cute, adorable, and worthy of special handling. Like you were.

GEORGE

Yes, special handling by the nannies. I lost count of them after a while. Rita saw each of them as a potential evil stepmother and most of them perceived Rita as the route to a marriage proposal from me. I only wanted a nanny for Rita. It's like those old photos in Cracker Barrel restaurants that you mentioned. Those people have no connection to you, they have no message for you. They are just inexpensively purchased decorations.

JILL

Like your ex-wife.

GEORGE

Inexpensively purchased, but believe me, I paid for it later.   She was expensive to send back.

JILL

Acquiring items from your childhood does not make you a child again. You can never go back there yourself.

Listen to Trudy.   You tell lies for a living, she does it for love.   The accumulated wisdom of women counts for far more than the ramblings of delusional men.   Unfortunately for humanity, the men controlled writing. Big mistake.

Think about these prophets, they thought that depriving themselves of food and water would bring enlightenment.   Doesn't happen at weight watchers, and didn't happen then.

If you lived here, I could be your agent.   That would be fun.

GEORGE

Oh boy! Now we have act three of your play.   You're finding me a wife, a second and possibly a third job, and Trudy is providing the home, well, it's really your home, and a family.

JILL

You've always had family, this is just a chance to appreciate it full time.   An inveterate traveler is like an affluent criminal fleeing his past.   You remind me of a wanted criminal who wants nothing more than to be recaptured. You should know that it is impossible to avoid reality.

GEORGE

Except here?

JILL

In many ways, yes. You can call it a work farm, or a green prison, or just home.

SCENE 3

(*Trudy, Brent, and Danielle together on the porch*)

TRUDY

These youngsters fondle their iPhone like true believers rubbing a fetish. Look at that preteen over there. She looks to be praying, hoping that her electronic prayer book will deliver to her the internet in its entirety. Or, lacking that, a simple text.

DANIELLE

She is persistent, I'll give her that.

TRUDY

But this is a pagan land, Brent. We have neither cell service nor Wi-Fi here. The electronic god has no power here, yet. If iPhone offered a nicotine app, thousands would die from exhaustion with their devices clutched like, like, a smoking revolver. Isn't that right Danielle? (*no response*)

Oh, to live in a world where I never need to touch another screened device.

DANIELLE

That world no longer exists.

TRUDY

The internet has become a library filled with nothing but fashion and gossip magazine. It's a huge electronic high school, frozen in recess.

I dream of the day that I'll read, maybe in a real made of paper newspaper, that some idiot has been killed in a gruesome internet accident. I can see the headline now

Bombastic moron spills beer, found electrocuted 3 days later. Moment of jolt uploaded as deceased man's last act. 4 million likes.

DANIELLE

As you can see Brent, Trudy is nothing if not pro internet.

TRUDY

When parents say don't drink, they really mean don't drink too much. It's the same advice about prospective marriage partners. What do you think?

DANIELLE

Where are we Trudy? You start too often in the middle of things. I'm not there with you inside your head. I'm a hitchhiker on this trip.

TRUDY

I'm sorry dear. You are absolutely correct. But your portion of the ride is over. Could you leave us for a few minutes, please? I'd like to chat with Brent and hear what stories he has for me. And I might even have one or two of interest for him. (*Danielle exits*)

I apologize for the melodrama, Brent. After so many years, the women in the family have a certain image of me. I have to maintain the persona of some mysterious seer. Otherwise they will be disappointed. I've become the character that they want of me.

BRENT

No worries, Trudy. Danielle advised me to be ready for anything.

TRUDY

I do the same with doctor, I pretend to believe that she is competent. It makes her feel important and shortens the visit. I go only if I need medicine.

BRENT

You don't have your prescriptions delivered?

TRUDY

Why would I? Getting out is exercise, seeing other people in flesh and blood is good for my health, although many of them seem to have more flesh than is healthy for them.

TRUDY

Danielle expects me to roar like a lioness. Oh yes, Brent, roaring is also for the queen of beasts

BRENT

Danielle tells me that you are the family powerbroker, but I'd use the word matriarch.

TRUDY

That's not sexist?

BRENT

Probably. Every utterance these days is sexist, or racist, for fascist. Maybe it depends on the meaning of ist. Ist is meaning less and less every day.

TRUDY

For some reason my disapproval is seen either as the seal of approval or as a dare by some of the members of the family.

BRENT

Danielle is among those. She is on pins and needles.

TRUDY

And you?

BRENT

Yes. For her sake, and what that means for our sake. She has shown me the family Button box, it is a unique method of remembering

TRUDY

I'd really like it if we could exchange some stories. Do you have any about your family that you'd like to share?

BRENT

Do I need to put a button in the box?

TRUDY

It isn't a parking meter. We usually ask guests to donate a button.

BRENT

Like boyfriends?

TRUDY

They have a poor track record.

BRENT

So do husbands in your family. (*pause*)

Family stories? About my father, none other than there was one, a father that is. It's a nonstory.

TRUDY

And your mother?

BRENT

My mother owns a bar and grill, it isn't fancy, but it has a pleasant atmosphere   My mother owns it now, but she used to work there as a barmaid.   I spent so many hours there as a kid, either at a table if it wasn't too crowded, or in back if it was. I was part time worker, and part mascot.

TRUDY

I see.

BRENT

No, you don't. I'm sorry, but I know what you are thinking, you asked for a story about my mother and I begin by talking about myself.

TRUDY

Many men can't progress beyond I.

BRENT

I'm only setting the scene so you would know that I saw an awful lot of the world in a bar and grill as an invisible kid. I'd like to finish my mother's story as if it were her telling it.
Her name is Becky, by the way.

(*continuing as his mother*)

Hipsters would say that it has a cool vibe, not quite hip, but cool. That is what a hipster would say, but they don't stop in. They avoid the suburbs. Before hipsters, back when I was just a barmaid, we called them young Turks, or yuppies. If they did stop by, it was only for a cheap night out. They were here only for the happy hour, and left their good manners locked in their beemers.

But we had some decent customers as well. They came for one or two, and were polite and tipped well. I remember one, his name was Reed, he was wealthy enough to afford honesty and smart enough to not get involved with women who didn't already share his last name. Reed asked me once what made our place so cool.

I said that we played music with understandable lyrics and that none of the barmaids, myself included, were lookers.

He was polite enough to fake embarrassment but curious enough to not change the topic.

I'm a plain woman, mirrors work for everyone.

I didn't mean, Reed stammered.

I'm not offended

You're very observant.

Us plain women are. (*pause*) Everything is a worry. (*pause*) Embarrassment doesn't become you. Relax, I've no time for games.

I find women in general to be observant.

Maybe. I don't know. I only speak for myself.

As a..

Yes, as a plain woman. I'm glad that we've settled that. I look around at my

Colleagues?

We are co-workers. None of us are educated enough to be addressed as colleagues.

You underestimate yourself.

I've picked up that habit from men, Reed. None of us are beauties, we have young, old, and in between. Its like peering into carnival mirrors, but instead of thin or thick, my mother would say fat, I become younger or older. But their image is mine. We even have the same T-shirt to wear as a uniform. We are, I know that this sounds silly, I'm not the one drinking, you are, but we are the same woman, the same non beautiful face, at different stages in one shared life. Wearing the same shirt doesn't help.

I was afraid that I'd scared Reed off as a customer, talking as I had, or that he was going to say something to the boss about me, so I did something that I'd rarely done before.

TRUDY

What did you do Becky? I mean, what did your mother do, Brent?

BRENT

Not what you are thinking Trudy. (*continuing as Becky*) I bought him a drink. I placed a bar chip in front of his nearly full glass. Another customer caught my attention, and by the time I got back to Reed, he'd left.

It was all quiet for a week or so, and then, one afternoon, Reed stops by with his wife.
We talk for a while, and he and she offer me

TRUDY

Offer you what?

BRENT

A chance to run and then own the bar. I only had one stipulation, we were going to burn those damned T-shirts.   (*continuing as Brent*) Reed gave me the very same bar chip years later, the one that my mother had placed before him that one day long ago. I'm hoping that Danielle will wear that at our wedding, see it's blue. (*pause*)

I think that it is your turn to tell me one of the Button stories. Its your serve.

TRUDY

Choose a button from the box. You are not superstitious?

BRENT

Not in the least.

TRUDY

That's a disappointment. And here I am, thinking that you are one of the smart ones.

BRENT

You're joking. I consider myself reasonably intelligent.

TRUDY

Superstition is simply another fashion of being alert and open to your senses. There are degrees to superstition, but to totally discount it shows a lack of perception. Go on, choose one.   It isn't like Tarot cards. Its just refreshing to let someone else choose, and it keeps my memory sharp. (*Brent chooses a small male cameo*)

This is an interesting one. Its made from Ivory, which is appropriate. This button was from Flick, I don't know if anyone knew his last name, or if he even had one. His parents had been former slaves. He had this tiny cameo button made from a sketch in a pre-civil war newspaper clipping advertising the sale of his father and family, that was the only image of his father and so he used that as his family album.

Imagine that, his entire family's history here, in one button. Think how lucky we are, we have nearly 200.

                           BRENT

So why is it here, among your family's history, if he wasn't family?

                           TRUDY

Flick was quite the character, I only knew him as a young girl, he was an old man by then of course. There aren't any pleasant alternatives to growing old, Brent. I remember overhearing him telling the adults, that he hadn't been the best of men, that he had committed most crimes, except murder and suicide.

                           BRENT

That's horrible, and yet he was permitted to stay. (*pause*) Oh, he meant it as a joke.

                           TRUDY

I think so. But no one was quite sure, which of course made it even funnier.

One day, Flick just disappeared, he left behind this button, no note as to what to do with it. I guess he didn't want to be a burden, either in life or in death. He accepted the burden of freedom better than anyone I ever met, before or afterward. Life demands a touch of sorrow as yeast. (*pause*)

You know, a few years ago, I visited the National Portrait Gallery in Washington. They had an entire section on cameos and silhouettes; they used to be very popular in the 19th century. That was before even my time, Brent.

I came across a framed newspaper page from the mid-1800s, and in it there was a silhouette of a male slave for sale, family included, $50. I like to think that maybe that was Flick's father, and that he'd found a family at last in the nation's capital.

BRENT

I've been to Washington several times, but only for work.

TRUDY

Danielle mentioned something about you having a summer job with the government.

BRENT

In a way. I might as well tell you the entire story. I remember hearing some of the customers at the bar reminisce about their college days. It was usually backpacking around Europe, traveling by train from one country to another. That used to be the thing to do. That or Tibet or Thailand. It was so baby boomer.

BRENT

I'm seeing my own country instead. I'm traveling by bus instead of rail. Maybe we will have trains someday.

TRUDY

Sure, right after they find Bigfoot

BRENT

I've been to 23 cities already

TRUDY

We have that many?

BRENT

St Louis, Seattle, Boston. I'm trying for Miami but it's not the season.

TRUDY

Not the season?

BRENT

For my summer job

TRUDY

Which is what, exactly? Bumming around the country by bus?

BRENT

Yes. Well I'll demonstrate.

TRUDY

You're going to demonstrate bumming around. I can envision it pretty easily.

BRENT

No my job is, I demonstrate. It is like uber or any other job in the so-called gig economy. I fit a certain demographic so I'm chosen to be part of a demonstration.

TRUDY

For what?

BRENT

For about $14 an hour, plus transportation of course. And some meals. Sometimes the meals are local cuisine but often it is just vouchers at McDonald's or Subway. Subway is the worst. I remember once

TRUDY

You are too young to begin recounting your memories

BRENT

One time we were protesting again a fast food chain and yet at the end of the day, we were given free coupons for the same chain

TRUDY

So, you are a paid demonstrator?

BRENT

Yep. It is interesting but it can also be boring.

TRUDY

Interesting but boring. That is the definition of a job.

BRENT

I've met and stayed with some nice people

TRUDY

You stayed with them?   Who are these nice people?

BRENT

Locals who are passionate about whatever it is that we are marching for, or against. We call them local color, or LC's.

TRUDY

Who is we, the demonstrators for hire?

BRENT

Yes, but we're known as demos.

TRUDY

Is everything is your lexicon an abbreviation or an acronym? So, you stay in the home of complete strangers?

BRENT

Sure. Why not? It's like a free air bnb. Rooms for rent in a house, a boarding house. You know, some of the demos are old. We call them

TRUDY

What?

BRENT

Never mind

TRUDY

No, I'd like to hear it.

BRENT

Retreads

TRUDY

How do you define old?

BRENT

Older than you.

TRUDY

Anyone older than me, I call fertilizer. It could be worse, I suppose. And you demonstrate for or against

BRENT

Sometimes both in the same day. That's difficult as I need a change of clothes. Social media and the iPhone can hurt my career. It is not a real career, you understand. Over exposure can really limit my marches. I have grown a beard for some assignments, or used a fake one if there isn't time between

TRUDY

Performances?

BRENT

Yes. I suppose you could call them performances.

TRUDY

You've been teasing me with this, haven't you? Have you and Danielle come up with this marvelous hoax of a story? Danielle is so wonderfully devious. As devious..

BRENT

As you?

TRUDY

I was going to finish my sentence by saying as devious as, her mother. But your ending works just as well. Me, Danielle, her mother, we are all devious.

BRENT

I hadn't noticed.

TRUDY

But what are you marching for?

BRENT

It doesn't matter. It's like here at the reunion. We play games whose outcome is of no importance. We can switch sides, reconstruct the teams, it's all in fun. We enjoy cake and wine afterwards.

TRUDY

Your wine is probably better.

BRENT

What I do is no different.

TRUDY

Hmm. You don't worry about violence?

BRENT

Well there is a premium for those who are willing to either give or take a hit, the first are called footballers, while the latter are soccers. I passed on both of those but the good news is that all of us are covered, at least by the big organizers, by health insurance.

TRUDY

This is surreal. Sane people really do this?

BRENT

Yes, hundreds of us. Its like working for Disneyworld, but we get to travel. It's a job, it pays better than OK, I am truly seeing my country, for better and worse.

I hope you don't think me as a black sheep of my family. Speaking of that, who is the black sheep of the Button family?

TRUDY

We have a farming background, we have an entire flock of them.

If you looking for the most notorious of them, the closest we have to a family villainess is cousin Merl. She left years ago using money she inherited from an uncle by marriage. There was always something strange between them. I was always told not to speak ill of the dead, especially if you don't know anything. Some here would make up some run of the mill gossip about him, May/December romance between a niece and her mother's sister's husband, but I don't support that. I prefer to assume the worst and believe if you can't say anything good about someone, you're better off accepting that they were more than likely a scumbag.

BRENT

That makes sense.

TRUDY

She was able to indulge her whims, doing whatever struck her fancy. I remember her saying once, "Je ne fait qu'à ma tête".

She does what she wants. Danielle said that to me about herself after we'd been dating for a while.

TRUDY

How did you respond to that?

BRENT

I haven't, not yet.

TRUDY

Merl spent a year or so in Paris. Another of her impulses, but one that I can't criticize. I wish that I had been able to done that myself.

I can't keep track of all her ventures, she never sticks to any one thing very long. Perfume, real estate, painter, restaurant. She is a pro at being an amateur, and an amateur at being professional.

BRENT

And she has failed at all of them? That is an old story. I expect that there was always a man there to bail her out?

TRUDY

Wrong on all counts. Her taste in men runs like mine does to coffee. I tried coffee a lifetime ago and decided that once was enough. I think that she had enough of whatever god forsaken perversion there was between her and Uncle Slimeball, may he rest in peace, and that she cut that portion of life from her life like a wart from her buttocks.

As far as her failing in her ventures, she was cursed with success. One of her competitors said in print that Merl strolled through life like she is starring in her own productions, and that he wished the supreme critic would drop the curtain early.

She succeeds at every enterprise. I will give you a recent example. She opened a small restaurant. It took off quickly, rave reviews, profitable beyond expectations. But it took too much of her time; having too many customers was a problem. So one day after hours, she calls the employees and tells them that they're done.

BRENT

That is harsh behavior, but then I don't know her.

TRUDY

You are correct, it is harsh. That is her way; she makes a decision, and boom, she is gone. Her spontaneity is more like spontaneous combustion to those who first experience it. She didn't even empty the restaurant's refrigerators.

BRENT

And the employees were just let go? No severance?

TRUDY

Absolutely there was a severance. She is punctilious about being fair is business. Her partners are never cheated, they just all feel that way afterward. Abandonment is the worst sin. It hurts the soul of the abandoned.

You have heard of the painting, La Joconde?

BRENT

Who hasn't? That is the French name for the Mona Lisa.

TRUDY

Yes. Millions of tourists flock to see it each year in the Louvre. But the rear side of the Mona Lisa is just gray canvas, the same as million other, unknown paintings.

Merl makes life look so carefree and easy, we call it the Happy Merl Movie. You will find that most us brag about her and hate her at the same time.

BRENT

The Button box for far more than only remembering, I think.

TRUDY

You concluded this on your own?

BRENT

Yes. Oh, you mean, did Danielle feed me that as a line to pass on to you? No, she didn't. In fact, the idea just popped into my head earlier, at the beginning of our sparring match. I'm not sure that she knows it herself.

TRUDY

And if you informed her of your discovery? Its not really a secret.

BRENT

She would realize immediately that it is true. It is a secret hidden in plain sight. The box is your own personal family Bible, filled with stories true and false, but not to be questioned because they are Button scripture. Ingenious. The box serves as a family icon shareable across generations. I understand what Danielle and George meaning that good stories can be both true and false. A la fois.

TRUDY

At the same time, yes. You are very observant Brent. I'm sure that the box started just as place to keep one off buttons, and then grew into something of worth. The castoff became the precious. It was not by design, but then life often isn't. It is still only a box with buttons of no practical use, but it has taken on a higher role.

BRENT

Life is a contact sport.

TRUDY

Recounting family stories is like filling in the dash between the dates on a tombstone.
The dead only matter in so far as they can contribute to the life of the current generation. We use their failures and successes as practical lessons. They give us unintended advice.

Americans can be hard parents. They take a lamaze class, but nothing beyond it. It's like leaving school after first grade. Parents improvise the most important role of their lives. Hell, they don't even need to audition before assuming the lead in a play that will run decades. It's dumb luck that any children survive to adulthood, where the repeat the same horrid play.

BRENT

To be blunt, we are all in the same play, I'm still in the first act, whereas you await the curtain.

TRUDY

Yes. We encourage children to move as soon and as far away as possible

BRENT

Like I'm doing. (*pause*) At least they return for these reunions. (*Tucker enters stage left*)
I think that we are done, aren't we? (*Trudy nods*).

TRUDY

I hope that you find us a satisfactory family, Brent. I'd enjoy seeing you at future reunions.

BRENT

So would I. I envy you a bit Trudy, living as you do in your lost 20th century hidden valley. Maybe it's mountains will protect you from the internet tsunami. Until the next time we see each other, Trudy. (*kiss on cheek*). Stay well. (*exits*)

TRUDY

(*turns to Tucker*) Did you get as far as Morgan's Rock?

TUCKER

Yes?

TRUDY

And?

TUCKER

Nothing. (*reaches into bag and pulls out button*). I took this with me, its Charlie's button.
I can put it back now, I'm safe. (*puts button back in the Button box*).

TRUDY

Safe from what? Why did Charlie's button keep you safe?

TUCKER

Safe from everything. I had a whistle too

TRUDY

But the button?

TUCKER

If anything bad happened, I knew that Gramps would come for the button, if not for me.

TRUDY

(*pause*) Tell me about Morgan's Rock.

TUCKER

It was fun. Maybe I'll write about it one day.

TRUDY

Your grandfather might be able to,

TUCKER

To what grandma?

TRUDY

I was going to say help, but that will come later. Listening. You grandfather might like to listen, he likes good stories.

TUCKER

Listening is helping, I think.

TRUDY

He likes good stories, and so do you.

TUCKER

That's because I'm a Button.

TRUDY

Yes, Tucker, you are a Button.

TUCKER

Do you think that gramps will let me keep him? (*opens bag*) Just until… my mom won't care either way, but until Gramps takes me back home.

TRUDY

A kitten, a beautiful kitten. I'm sure that your Gramps will let you keep him. Does your kitten have a name?

TUCKER

If it was a girl cat, I would call her Morgan, that is where I found him, but since he's a boy and I found him during the reunion, I was thinking of naming him Button, just Button.

SCENE 4

DANIELLE

You did well with Aunt Trudy.

BRENT

And if I hadn't

DANIELLE

If you hadn't, I might even sic Aunt Joyce on you, she hasn't been fed in a while. She might decide that to take you for a quick roll in the hay. It would be literally a roll in the hay; you've already taken a tour of the barn. She has the hungry look, as I said it's been awhile since she's dined

I didn't really speak with Joyce much, I just listened. She has the eyes of a

DANIELLE

Cougar

BRENT

That was too easy Danielle. I would have said cat.

DANIELLE

She probably had the intense gaze that she does when she is famished.

BRENT

What about her husband?

DANIELLE

They died.

BRENT

They? How many did she have?

DANIELLE

A few, some, several. More than one. Does it matter? They weren't concurrent, if that's what is bothering you.

BRENT

Nothing is bothering me, I'm just trying to get the lay of the land

DANIELLE

And you think that might be Joyce?

BRENT

No! It was just an expression.

DANIELLE

I'm just teasing about you and Joyce. I said that you were safe we me, and you are.

BRENT

That's a relief. She is very nice...

DANIELLE

For a nymphomaniac; I wasn't teasing about that. Just because she is sick doesn't mean that she isn't able to hunt.

BRENT

And the sequence of husbands?

DANIELLE

Nor about that. In fact, her most recent husband, Winston, did just recently die

BRENT

From a heart attack, in bed, I suppose?

DANIELLE

One would think that, knowing Joyce, but no, it was just natural causes. By the way, her daughter Tracie is the same way.

BRENT

I noticed.

DANIELLE

Well, if you have a chance to speak with her again, don't.

BRENT

Ok, I won't. May I ask why not?

DANIELLE

Let's just say that you wouldn't find either Tracie or her mother in a convent. Worse, Tracie doesn't respect family boundaries as well as her mother.

BRENT

Attending a Button reunion is quite an educational field trip.

DANIELLE

With her, you would be unlikely to survive the hay mow; either she'd kill you during the roll, or I would kill you afterward.

BRENT

I take your point; dying happy or dying unhappy is still dying

DANIELLE

I was going to tell you a funny story about her late husband Winston.

BRENT

Dead husbands can certainly be droll. Your Aunt Joyce must have enough material to do a standup act on a Carnival cruise ship.

DANIELLE

I think she tried that once. It didn't end well for anyone. So, getting back to Winston. He was well off enough even in retirement.

BRENT

Retired from what?

DANIELLE

Once you're retired, retired from what becomes an inane question. It's like asking what you were before you were born. After retirement, he continued with his past time of carpentry; he was really quite skilled. And modest.

Modest, skilled, and probably decent in bed; I can see why Joyce married him.

BRENT

And why did Winston marry him? Is she immodest, highly unskilled but spectacular in bed?

DANIELLE

You will never find out.

BRENT

Is it reasonable to speculate that opposites attract?

DANIELLE

You are catching on. Winston redid almost every wood fixture in their house, moldings, doors, cabinets. I never saw any of this until the day of Winston's wake; Joyce held it her house.

BRENT

Where is the funny part, up to this point it is much more sad than humorous

DANIELLE

Years before, Winston had a premonition that once he had finished the kitchen cabinets he was going to die.

BRENT

Like the woman owner of Winchester House?

DANIELLE

Exactly.   But for him is was not quite the expense it was for the proprietor of Winchester; he simply needed to do nothing; just simply not hang the doors. They remained in the basement for who knows how long, several years at least.

BRENT

You are telling me that these cabinet doors are complete, all finished and ready for hanging, but there they sit in the basement all because of a dream?

DANIELLE

Yes.

BRENT

But despite his abiding by the "rules",   Winston died anyway?

DANIELLE

Yes.

BRENT

Where is the humor in that?

DANIELLE

We held Winston's wake at Joyce's house, mostly in the kitchen. Few of us had ever been there before, but it was so easy to find cups, and spoons, and sugar.

BRENT

On account of there not being any doors on the cabinets? That is funny.

DANIELLE

One of Winston's not close, creepy friends, Ian I think, mentioned that he'd be happy to come over one day the following week and install the cabinet doors for Joyce. We all knew what he really wanted to hang, Joyce included, but she was too polite to decline his offer.

BRENT

Don't tell me that they are now...

DANIELLE

An item? Like us? Not hardly. Do you see him with her now?

BRENT

No, I don't see that she is with anyone. But husbands around here seem to have a short shelf life.

DANIELLE

Winston's friend, Ian stopped by Joyce's the following week, went down to the basement and started to bring the cabinet doors up. He must have tripped, he fell halfway down the stairs and broke his neck.

BRENT

Dead?

DANIELLE

Unhappy dead or happy dead is still dead. D E A D, dead.

SCENE 5

TRUDY

I am exhausted, Jill. You must be even more tired than I am.   I'm just
going to sit here a little longer and enjoy the peace. There are going to be
some big changes around here.

JILL

You didn't tell George, then?

TRUDY

No, I didn't need to. He came around at the end.   He's finally learned the
same lesson that young Brent has: his decisions should be made by him.

JILL

It's just up to us to lead our men to believing that myth. (*pause*)   And
Danielle, did you tell her about George's marriage?

TRUDY

Nope. Its a lesson that she has learned all by herself. Danielle is a natural.

JILL

Do you think that there is a future for George and Anna? I really would like
to find another husband.

TRUDY

I hope so. I owe him.

JILL

But he owes you more. If you hadn't found a boyfriend for George's ex-wife, George and Shannon

TRUDY

Sophie

JILL

They'd still be married. And George would never have written anything of value. And I'd never have had the chance to remodel this old house. (*George and Tucker and Button enter stage right*).

FIN

www.ingramcontent.com/pod-product-compliance
Lightning Source LLC
Chambersburg PA
CBHW031311280626
47169CB00017B/1192